MW01487762

Hot and Heavy
Erotica Stories

*About Dirty Sex, BDSM,
Threesomes, Anal, and
All Your Wildest
Fantasies*

Anya Coxx

cannot amend, distribute, sell, use, quote or paraphrase any part, or the content within this book, without the consent of the author or publisher.

<u>Disclaimer Notice:</u>

Please note the information contained within this document is for educational and entertainment purposes only. All effort has been executed to present accurate, up to date, reliable, complete information. No warranties of any kind are declared or implied. Readers acknowledge that the author is not engaged in the rendering of legal, financial, medical, or professional advice. The content within this book has been derived from various sources. Please consult a licensed professional before attempting any techniques outlined in this book.

By reading this document, the reader agrees that under no circumstances is the author responsible for any losses, direct or indirect, that are incurred as a result of the use of the information contained within this document, including, but not limited to, errors, omissions, or inaccuracies.

Table of Contents

To Protect and Serve

    Chapter 1: The Prick

    Chapter 2: To Whore, or Not to Whore

    Chapter 3: The Decision

    Chapter 4: Date Night

Three Is a Party

    Chapter 1: 7-Day Trial

    Chapter 2: The Scale

    Chapter 3: One Last Attempt

    Chapter 4: The Meeting

The More the Merrier

    Chapter 1: The Invitation

Chapter 2: Scheme

Chapter 3: Presentation Is Everything

Chapter 4: The Covenant

Between the Cheeks

Chapter 1: Sugar and Spice

Chapter 2: Exit Only

Chapter 3: Practice Makes Perfect

Chapter 4: All or Nothing

A Night with Paris

Chapter 1: The Gorilla

Chapter 2: Size Is Everything

Chapter 3: A Trick or a Treat

To Protect and Serve

Chapter 1: The Prick

Shit, it was going to be another long night. My last table was still sitting there, camping the bill, and I was stuck sitting there, waiting until they were ready to call it a night. I could've tried to be passive about it. Maybe walk over and say, *"Oh, I didn't realize you haven't placed your credit or debit card down yet. I'll be back to take care of it for you shortly."* Maybe that would've got them to pay. I just wanted to get out of there. Still had other tables to buss, ring in my tips for the night, tip out the hostess and bartender, and--*DING!*

I glanced over at Mary as she approached the front counter to seat some gentleman. "Would you like to sit at a table or the bar?" she asked him. The man tucked his glasses into his brown coat and staggered against the counter to help stand on his own two feet. *What a whackjob. Who walks into a bar already fucked up? I mean, look at him.* His button-down shirt missed half of the buttons. His black disheveled hair barely stood in place as he swaggered back and forth. I'd say the only thing that looked right about him were his bright, blue eyes, then again, even those were trying to hide behind his drooping eyelids.

"I want the bar. Then table." He hiccuped. "I'm hungry." Mary grabbed a menu for him.

"Follow me, sir." She then led him to the bar and placed the menu down. He took his place, and Angela placed a napkin down in front of him, along with a list of the night's specialty drinks.

"What can I get for ya?" Angie asked him. I folded clothes for tomorrow night's dinner, hoping I'd eventually see what table he'd like to sit at. Hoping it wasn't mine.

"Your number," he answered, barely able to muddle the words from his lips.

"Excuse me?" His voice carried throughout the restaurant. Other customers heard his request and shook their heads at his drunken attempt of flirtation.

"You heard me, lady. Your number. You're 'pose to get me…" He hiccuped again. "What I want…ain't that right?"

"I'll get you a water." *Good job, Angie.* She didn't say a word more or allow him to stop her.

When she returned, she placed a water glass before him.

"Gracie?" my manager called. When I turned to him, he exhaled. "Listen, I'm sorry to have to do this to ya, but we need you a bit longer tonight."

"Come on, Rich, really?"

"I'm sorry. We got people coming in from the Brewers' game. It's good business. Besides, I heard you could use the tips." *Damn it.* He wasn't wrong there. I've been holding this job as best as I can just to be able to make the minimum payments for college tuition, yet struggled to pay that already.

"Alright, Rich. Sounds good." He nodded.

After I cleaned my other tables, adjusted my settings at my station how they should be, and made sure all of the garbage in the front stations of the restaurant were taken out, I found that Angie had sat the man down at my station. Yeah. It was going to be a long night.

I gave him time to scan over the menu, probably more than enough time the average person needed because this wasn't your average person. This was a drunken, horny, butt-fuck testing his pick-up skills, and he probably thinks that just because he's drunk, he won't be corrected for his remarks.

When I approached the table, I noticed he hadn't taken a sip of his water yet. A frustration was already building inside of me, burrowed deep in my gut, welling itself up my windpipe, and trapping itself in my throat. I got my pen and paper ready, hoping he'd stop me midway and tell me what he wanted so I can get his table turned as quickly as possible to get out of there.

"Good evening. My name is Gracie, and I'm going to be taking care of you tonight? Would you like anything to drink besides water for now?"

I was surprised he didn't stop me or say much. All he did was shake his head, then pointed at his water glass.

"Alright, would you like more time on the menu, or are you all set to order?"

"You in a rush there, cupcake?" I refrained from responding, trying not to stir his pot and get him going before he overflown and spewed out a ridiculous attempt of a compliment that would really be an insult. "Don't worry; I won't keep you long. You must want to get home."

Should I be honest or polite? I mean, he didn't have any politeness himself, and he certainly didn't deserve it. However, in my profession, no matter what person walks through that door, you give everyone the same respect and service as the next...

"Actually, sir, I am. I am trying to get home." Honesty won the tug of war, after all. A smirk creased up the sides of his face, and for a moment, he looked a bit younger than I had expected him to be the way he staggered through the door. Couldn't be much older than myself if he fixed his hair and wore some different threads. This guy might have had a real chance with a little adjustment to his game.

"When you go home, you should take me with you." He winked. I gripped tighter around the pen and started tapping its end on the pad.

"I'm afraid I'm not interested, sir."

"Oh, trust me." *And. Here. We. Go.* "I can convince you otherwise."

"You might want to convince me you want to order something, or I'll be closing out early tonight… Sir." Once he spotted my frustration, the look on his face relaxed and he nodded. He took a deep sigh, scanned over the menu, then held out it out for me to take.

"I'll just stick with the water for now. I'll let you know if I need anything." I conjured up a smile, trying to swallow down the anger rising inside of me, but it just wouldn't go down. He was going to purposely keep me waiting on him just to torture me. I started to think I probably should have been nicer to him. Just stuck to being polite, and he would have ordered something and been on his way. I collapsed to a sit, throwing my face into my hands, trying not to pout. Angie came over and moved some of my brown strands from my face and shook her head.

"That long of a night, huh?"

"That guy." I shook my head. "He's going to make me lose it."

"Get him in and get him out. Control the table." We looked over at the table, and the moment I made eye contact with him, he raised his empty water glass and pointed at it.

"Looks more like he's taking control of *me.*"

Angie held out the water pitcher, and I took it from her and hurried over to the table. *Take control. Just take control. Just another drunk. He's no different than any other person that walks through the door.* I grabbed his glass, but he kept his grip on the bottom and smiled. He then released it when he saw I wasn't going to attempt to battle with him. I poured the water, and as I watched it fill the glass, I couldn't help but feel his eyes eating away at my body. I turned away from him to leave, but before I could leave, he grabbed me by the wrist. Any other time, I might have whipped around and socked him in the eye. But the way he grabbed it, it wasn't a tight grip. He didn't pull. It was as if he thought my wrist was made of glass. I felt frozen where I stood, still not turning back to him. I took a breath, and he released me.

"I'm sorry," he said, and he actually sounded sincere. Maybe the water was finally coming to my rescue. Maybe not. I turned to him and decided to hear him out. Being polite would get him out. "Sorry for being a pest. It's been a long day and night."

I nodded. "Yes." I agreed with him for sure. "It has been a long night."

"Would be nice to have someone to talk to." He ran his hand back across the top of his head and against the sides and conjured up a friendly smile. Not that freakish glare or male-gaze he had all night. The real him seemed to finally show. I leaned against the side of his table and folded my arms over my chest. I scanned around the restaurant as other waiters and waitresses started clearing their tables and cashing out their tips. It wasn't like I had other customers to check on, and I had a great feeling he knew that as well.

"What is it you'd like to talk about?"

"You."

"What about me?"

"Well, tell me something about you, I can't see."

"And what is it that you see?"

"Beautiful, long, brown hair. Hazel eyes. Perfect tan. Not sure if it's all over." He smiled, then it faded when I didn't join his laughter. "Long legs. Might be as tall as me if I stand up again to remember." I shrugged. "Why a restaurant? Why work here when you can be cat-walking in fashionable clothes with models, having people like me throw you roses and kiss your feet." I almost laughed out loud, but I threw my fingers over my lips.

Throw me roses and kiss my feet? From people like him? But most of all, me? A model? Yeah. Okay, buddy. His smooth moves were starting to show themselves as well.

"I work here because it's the only place I have experience that's close to my apartment."

"You saving? Young, beautiful woman like yourself should be saving up for something nice to put up with this--," and he looked around the restaurant, "--nice place." He meant shithole.

"I can't save. I'm paying my way per semester for school. I don't make enough to save."

"Sounds like you could use a new job."

I chuckled. "I guess, but as I've said, I--"

"I could help you with that. You know, I could pay your tuition for you." Pay my tuition for me? He didn't even know the price, let alone, seem like the type to be more than half a tax bracket above me.

"Just to humor you, what exactly would I have to do?" He downed his water and held it up for another pour. As I poured, that fiendish smirk returned, and the good guy I started to sense within him faded.

Chapter 2: To Whore, or Not to Whore

The drunk has risen. If this was his way of telling me that as long as I kept his water glass full and placed an order for him, if he was going to make one, that he'd give a great tip, then it wasn't convincing me.

"So, I just have to listen to you?" He nodded. "But I already am. I'm here, aren't I? Giving you water no matter how many times you hold it up and decide not to use your words like a child." He chuckled to himself, but nothing I said sounded close to being funny. He could have been laughing at himself, realizing that I was calling him exactly how he was acting – a child.

"It's not that simple."

"Then be specific. You're so vague, and I have to say, you seem less vague when you're trying to give a compliment."

"Have a seat." He motioned for me to sit across from him. I took my place without contesting, just to humor him longer and see how far he actually gets.

"What now, master?" I mumbled.

"That actually sounded pretty good." I frowned and tried not to laugh. Oh, I got it. A perv. He's more a prick than a perv. How could I not have possibly guessed that? I chuckled from my own hilarity, and he smiled with amusement.

"By pretty good, you mean you want me to call you master for the rest of the night?"

"You're so fixed on the here and now, Gracie, and need to start thinking ahead. I don't want you to just call me master *tonight*. I want you to call me master *in bed*. How about some...bondage." I slapped him. The smack sounded throughout the restaurant, but we both looked around, and no one else seemed to notice what happened besides seeing us sitting there looking back at them.

"That felt pretty good," he said.

"Yeah, it sure as hell did feel good," I told him. "Care for another?"

"Not here."

"You're disgusting." He smiled again...And kind of cute. I kind of did like his hair all messy, yet he kept fixing it. "You want to take me home and be your whore?" He shook his head in disgust.

"No, not at all. That's--that's completely absurd. Unless you're into that sort of thing?"

"What? Absolutely not."

"Well, good. That's not what I was offering."

"Then what are you offering besides money?"

"A great time. You come home with me and listen to what I say," he ran a finger from my elbow, up to my wrist, and I removed my arms from the table and tucked my hands between my thighs. "--and you won't have to worry about your tuition."

If he wasn't so hands-on in public, I might have actually considered his offer. Making me feel like some public plaything was not the way inside of me. Though, his persistence was a bit sexy, but still. *He's a fucking pervy prick.*

"So, Gracie, what do you say?" How could I have possibly took a moment to even think about it? Sure, I needed the money, but how did I know he even had it? "I can give you half now and half after."

"Because you carry around almost four grand in your pocket?"

"Who can fit four grand in their pocket?" He tapped his water glass. I felt he was sobering himself up without any issues. I poured him more. When his hand gripped around the glass, I eyed his golden ring.

"You're married?" I almost jumped out of my seat. He eyed his wedding band and twirled it around his finger with his thumb.

"I *was.*"

"Lucky woman," I said with sarcasm.

"No, I was a lucky man."

"I'm guessing she found out about your peculiar sexual tastes, and it drove her away."

"No, she didn't run away from me."

"What'd she do?"

"She died." *Shit. Great job, Gracie. Way to go.*

"I'm--I'm sorry. I didn't--"

"Know. Don't worry. I've healed from it." I didn't think of asking what happened and instead, figured if we stuck to what he wanted to talk about, it would clear the air.

"About this...offer."

"Have you decided?"

"I haven't. It's tempting, but-
-"

"But what? A man is offering to pay your tuition for just

one fun night, and you turn it down?"

"Listen, my body doesn't have a price. Especially for bondage."

"Everything--"

"Has a price, yes, I've heard the saying, but my body isn't one of them."

"Don't think of it that way. That may be the reason why you can't decide, wondering if you're breaking your moral code, or would this make you some 'whore' as you put it. Whatever happened to just enjoying *your* life? Not giving a damn what others think. Doing what's in your best interest."

"How is doing this my best interest?"

"I could pay you enough that will take care of your tuition and let you live comfortably for a while." Now *that* sounded tempting. This lottery ticket just walked into the restaurant, willing to pay this much money for a *fun* night? I exhaled and shook my head. I can't. No matter how tempting it is. I just-- can't. Besides, this can all be words. Just another way for him to waste my time since I've been rude to him. Twice. I rose from the chair, and his face lifted in surprise.

"Is there anything else I can get for you tonight?" He frowned and studied me then shook his head.

"No, Gracie. That will be all. I'll take the bill." I nodded and left him there as he finished his glass of water. As I prepared his bill at the register, Angie walked over, confused, and clocked her watch.

"Jesus, you two were talking for a while. What *did* you two talk about?"

"Some job offering that could pay for my tuition and more."

"And you said no?"

"Hell yes, I said no." But I forgot that Angie had no clue of the job title and description.

"Listen, I've seen you struggling, and it breaks my heart that I can't help you myself. Whatever job it is that he's offering, for that much money, must be worth at least considering. I mean, if it were me, I'd do *anything* to live comfortably and be out of this hellhole."

"Thanks, Angie. I really do appreciate it, but I don't know. I just...I just can't." I ripped his check from the machine and placed it into a book.

"Well, then you'll be working here for as long as Richie has, and he's been here ever since his hair was all black. Now he barely has any at all." I sighed as she walked away. Maybe if she knew more about what the job was, she wouldn't say such things. Or, maybe she still would be. If she were me, Angie probably would have taken that job, but I'm not Angie.

I returned to his table with the checkbook and placed it down in front of him. He immediately reached into his wallet to pay.

"I'm sorry, um..." and I didn't realize I never got his name. "I just can't do it. I'm used to taking orders."

"Then you fit the job description," he said. "I'm required to give them." He placed five-hundred-dollar bills on his thirty-dollar check of drinks he had at the bar. Before he closed his wallet, a golden badge which read, *Chief of*

Police gleaned in my eye. "If you decide to change your mind, there's more where that came from." He left his police card atop of the cash, and without another word, he walked casually out of the restaurant.

Chapter 3: The Decision

"He finally left," Angie said as she cashed out her tips.

"Yeah, he did."

"And you let him leave." She shook her head. "You're crazy, Gracie."

"You have no idea what he was offering." Richie looked over and squinted as he handed Angie her tips.

"It wasn't a new job, was it?" he asked.

"Richie, I'm not going anywhere," I assured him. I, at least, didn't plan on working at the restaurant as long as he had either. He smiled and nodded.

"Alright, just checking because we'd hate to see you go." As he left me and Angie there, we rolled our eyes and shook our heads. *Keep telling yourself that, Richie.* Angie sighed then eyed the clock.

"Need a ride home?"

"Yeah, please."

"Maybe along the way you can tell me about this job offer."

We gathered our coats and hats for the rain. Whenever it rained, the worms came out to eat at the restaurant. I was always thankful for the rainy days. It gave good money that went towards my tuition. On days it didn't rain in Webster, I'd work doubles to make up for it. Around this time of year, late Spring, when the sun started to show itself again, it was a double every other day. When we got to the car, Angie wiggles her fingertips on a ballsack decoration she had hanging from her rearview mirror.

"What the fuck?" I couldn't help but laugh.

"What? It gives good luck. I swear."

"Caressing your fingers on that thing does not give good luck."

"Maybe that's what you and your friend need to get into." She started the engine and jammed it into drive.

"Well, since you brought it up, that's exactly what he might have liked for me to do. Some-- kinky bondage shit." Angie smirked and shook her head.

"Wait, what? He did not?"

"Uh, yeah, he did."

"He wants you to caress his balls and would pay your tuition?"

"Crazy, right?"

"Crazy that you said no!" I shook my head and peered out of the window at the rain pounding against the glass, drowning every house and business we passed. "That man only asked for you to give his sack some love, and in return, he'd take care of you. You're insane."

"He wanted me to 'take orders' and even said--" and I tried to mimic his deep, throaty voice that was pestered in beer, "--I'm required to give them.'"

"That sounds sexy."

"That sounds insane! Perverted!"

"Look." We came to a red light, and it beamed through the windshield. "Gracie, he might have been a bit of a drunk, but you have to admit, that messy look and hazy, male-gaze just--ugh! I'd fix him up so good."

"Get out of here!" I kept laughing.

"I would've rode that hunk like a fucking jackrabbit." Angie started bouncing her ass up and down in her seat like she was squat-riding him. "Yes! Fuck me! Tie me up! Smack my ass! Gag-ball me!"

Another car pulled up with a bunch of guys. I sunk into my seat and put my hand to my face, yet couldn't keep myself from laughing. The horn honked.

"Hey! You girls want to come with us!" They continued to cat-call as Angie rolled down her window.

"The fuck are you doing?" I whispered.

"My friend would like to, she--" And I pulled her away from the window and fought her to step on the gas. When she was finally able to laugh, after I tried to suffocate her, she stepped on it and continued driving down the road. Her laughter thundered around me.

"I'm sorry, but you seriously need some in your life."

"Some *what*, Angie?" Already knowing exactly what she meant.

"Dick, Gracie! Dick! Must I spell it out for you? D-I-C-K. DI-_"

"I get it. I get it. Dick," I laughed. When our laughter finally calmed, she sighed and pulled into my apartment complex driveway. She put the car in park and ran her hand through her hair, then rested back in her seat.

"On a serious note, it is something to think about. I mean, make sure the guy is clean. Use a condom. Spit and swallow." We chuckled. "But, at least give him a call. Think of it as a second interview."

"Goodbye, Angie." She laughed as I got out of the car. I watched from the window as she pulled off, still holding the officer's card in my hand. Chief Duke Wells. Chief Wells. I like Duke better.

I spent all night studying his card to memorization, from the curves of the print-form badge to the letters in his name to his phone number. I paced back and forth in the kitchen in my nightgown, still reading it. I should not have been even considering contacting him, but something compelled me. I found myself removing my laptop from my bag and opening it on my bed. I logged into my school account online.

Balance Due: $3,798.68

**Payment Arrangement:
$362/week.
Past Due Amount: $265.08**

I was already late on my previous payment. Two weeks longer, and my classes would be dropped. It was getting close, and the money I made tonight still didn't cover both my current payment and the past due amount. I was desperate. I opened the Phone tab on my iPhone and hovered my thumb over a number. I couldn't call him, not fully understanding what I was getting into. So, instead, I had to give myself a bit of an interview beforehand.

I laid my fur pillow back and fluffed it up more with a few pats. I removed my vibrator from beneath the pillow next to it and relaxed back. It had been a while since I've mustered the energy to please myself.

When I felt relaxed enough, I curled my fingers around the bottom of my gown and lifted the gown until it exposed my purple silk panties. I pulled the computer close to my side and navigated through my bookmarks to PornHub.

When the site opened, previews of porn videos played in different rows and columns, each with its own category from ANAL to BIG DICKS to EBONY to MILFs to LESBIAN/BI. But I hovered the cursor over BDSM. The preview showed a woman tied up in ropes, suspended from the floor, her nipples pinched by what looked like jumper cables, and her mouth holding a red gag ball as if she were a roasted pig. She had tears coming down her eyes that drowned her face in milky, black makeup. It looked painful, but I guess to some, it was a pleasure.

I found the courage to press the button, and as the page loaded, a much bigger video picture, I powered my vibrator and rested it against my love pearl behind my panties, right between the lips. The moment the buzz touched me, a gasp escaped my lips, almost sending my eyes into the back of my head. My legs jolted, almost knocking into each other at the knee, but I forced myself to keep my legs open.

When the video loaded, the man was slapping her ass with a skinny, thin whip. Red marks flashed against her butt cheeks, but when he removed her gag-ball, she started begging for him to fuck her. I thought she'd beg for him to stop, but she wanted quite the opposite. He held her face in his hand, then pushed her face away.

I grinded against the vibrator, feeling a warm wetness build from inside of me. As it tried to find its way from between my lips, the man approached the woman from behind, adjusted her ropes so that her ass was directly in front of his black dress pants, and he kept pulling her against his crotch, teasing her.

I slid my panties to the side and put the tip of the vibrator inside of me, squeezing around its girth with a tight grip, keeping my pre-cum inside of me. The man then pulled down his pants as the woman begged. *Fuck me. Please. Please. Please. Fuck me.* And he shoved his thick, pink cock inside of her. Her eyes rolled in the back of her head, she tossed her head to the ceiling, and she moaned with each thrust he shoved inside of her. Her ass clapped against his muscular thighs, her hair danced atop her head, and when he pulled back and removed his cock, she started squirting all over the floor. I couldn't help but let some of my own cum drip out of me and onto my bedsheets. It wanted to come out so I let it.

My vibrator drowned inside of me, as it throbbed against my clit, and massaged my kitty inside out. He slapped her ass over and over, making it redder, then approached her mouth and shoved his cock inside her throat. She gagged and choked, the spit and tears dripped from her chin. I felt my climax building, getting hot. Throbbing like a heart in my vagina, but before I could cum, my iPhone rang.

I jolted up in bed and seen Angie's name appear. I quickly clicked out of the porn site, fixed my panties over my hips, and turned off the vibrator.

"Hello," I answered.

"Jesus, Gracie, you sound out of breath. You working out?" I managed to chuckle and shrugged.

"Something like that. What's going on?"

"Did you call that guy yet?"

"No." I checked his card again. "No, I haven't."

"Well, what are you waiting for?!" After what I witnessed, I was unsure myself. The BDSM looked sexy to watch but to actually be bound and tied up like that, having a cock shoved into my mouth, barely able to breathe out my own nose filled with spit and tears and makeup, seemed like an entirely different experience.

"Well, maybe, I will."

"Do it, and afterward, you can tell me what happened."

"Alright. Talk to you soon." We hung up, and I studied Duke's card again. Just do it, Gracie. What do you have to lose? Well, my dignity. My pride. Those things are priceless, but perhaps it was the thrill-ride I watched that conditioned me to call him anyway.

"Hello?" His throaty voice said when he answered. It took me a while to answer back. It's like I almost forgot that when someone says hello, you say it back to let them know you're there. "Hello? Who is this?"

"Hi, um, Duke. It's Gracie."

"Gracie? Oh, hey. Good to hear your voice again, especially at this time of night."

"Yeah. Um, yours too." And it was. "I considered what you

said."

"And?"

"And um. I don't know what I'm doing really I just--"

"Don't worry. I'll guide you along the way. Are you available now?"

"Now?" And I was. I was already dripping wet through my panties, so if there was any better time to finish, it was to let him do it for me. "Now is--fine. Yeah. Um."

"I'll host," he said, "but text me your address."

"Okay, I'll do that."

"And Gracie?"

"Yes?"

"Don't wear any panties."

Chapter 4: Date Night

When he arrived, he didn't honk. Instead, he sat in front of my complex apartment. How did I know he was here? Because he arrived in his cop car with the lights flashing as if it were an actual emergency call. I thought he might have been taking it too seriously, or perhaps I was taking it too lightly. I thought of what he said and removed the panties from beneath my gown. I threw on black heels instead, hoping that even though I didn't know what to expect from all of this, heels would at least suffice my way of trying to be sexy. I threw my black coat on over my gown to keep from cold. It was still raining that night, and it would suck to catch a cold.

I stepped out into the rain, and there he was in his police chief outfit, propped against the door of his car. What had me confused is that when I approached him, I realized he had the handcuffs in his hands.

"Happy to see me?" I asked him, thinking he'd say something smooth.

"Actually, Gracie, you're under arrest." *What?!* He grabbed me by the arm and turned me around, then bent me over the hood of his wet police car. The metal thudded against me, and the rain drowned my gown in the front. My cold, nipple hard breasts could pierce through the metal to the engine, but if it actually could, I hoped it would seduce him from arresting me.

"You tricked me!" Lights turned on from other apartments throughout the complex. He threw my wrists behind my back and cuffed me.

"You're under arrest for prostitution, Miss Gracie." I struggled in his grasp, trying to free myself. If I could free myself and make it inside my apartment, I'd lock the door and claim it was sexual harassment from the chief of police himself.

"I can't believe you!" He then caressed his fingers up my gown and massaged open-handed against my pussy lips and spread them with his fingers.

"This is all a part of the fun, Gracie," he whispered in my ear. I then relaxed beneath him, trying to muster up a smile. It was all a part of it. The roleplay. "Are you that wet, or is it the rain?"

I mustered the confidence to play along.

"Why don't you try and find out," I said. He removed his hand, then pulled me off of the car and threw me into the backseat.

"Next time you resist arrest, Miss Gracie, I'll have to get physical."

"I'm sorry, Duke," I said, with a flirt in my voice.

"It's chief."

"I mean, Chief. I'm sorry, Chief. I'll be good." He smirked and closed the door. The entire ride to his house, he didn't say much. He clocked me through the rearview mirror, looking as stern as possible. This couldn't have possibly been the same guy who came into the restaurant earlier that evening. But it was. Same male gaze, only his hair was slicked beneath his hat, and he looked much younger than he did in uniform.

He drove us up a hill that led to a luxurious white house. I started to rethink the career I had chosen for myself. I didn't think a police chief could have possibly made this much from the force, but once the thought of his wife dying crossed my mind, I realized where the money must've come from and where my mind should not be venturing. He pulled me out into the rain.

"I thought you were taking me downtown...Chief."

"Down to my bed, if that's what you meant." He kept me bound with the cuffs. They were a bit tighter than I thought he should have them, but perhaps part of this roleplay included some pain. A little pain now and then is fine, just as long as he kept this interesting.

Already he was making me forget that I had just met him hours ago.

His house had many see-through windows, and I wondered which one did he plan on throwing me up against. All of them? That would suffice. If they were strong enough to keep me from breaking through them, he could toss and turn my ass over as much as he would like.

When we got inside, I couldn't help but feel myself wanting him more. He took his time taking off his hat, removing his boots, unbuttoning his shirt just enough for me to see the stubble on his chest. He then placed his hat atop my head. He uncuffed me so he could remove my coat, but then he put the cuffs back on, and this time, it did hurt.

"Too tight?" he asked. I fought the pain, trying to be as

strong and willing as the woman I saw on the porn site. I shook my head.

"Not as tight as me." He licked his lips and pressed his stubble beard against my face. He might have known I would call him because his beard smelled of a masculine, beard shaving cream scent. It was alluring. Hypnotizing. I trembled in his grip, trying to keep myself from melting to the floor.

He led me upstairs and to the bedroom. The gigantic bed with thick, white cushions and pillows centered the room with wide, wall-to-wall, floor-to-ceiling windows that showed the outside forest of trees before they met the main road. He threw me onto the bed, face down, and I heard his belt buckle click. It flopped to the floor, and before I could muster any words as to what he was going to do to me, he spread my cheeks apart and slithered his tongue inside of my pussy. He licked the wetness I had since I watched the video, and he groaned as he ate me off his beard. The smacking and licking only made me shudder, and as I tried to close my legs, he spread me open once more.

"Stop resisting," he said, and his breath touched every inch of my skin down there, making me shudder even more. The dampness from the rain on my gown weighed heavy on my back. He crawled on top of me and ripped it as if it were a piece of paper. I couldn't possibly be mad. This sexual craving he had seemed monstrous, and I wanted this monster to devour me inside and out.

He curled my legs beneath me, so I was kneeling on the bed

with my face against the cover. He smacked my ass, and the smack echoed against the glass windows. I would have thought it could shatter it. He didn't talk much. Just like the guy in the video. He must've knew what he was doing. He must've known that telling a girl what a man was going to do is completely different than actually doing it. He simply acted on all of his thoughts, I assumed, for his tongue and lips were all over me, kissing down my back until he reached my tailbone. He licked there. And sucked there. Then ate me out again from behind, digging his thumb into my ass as he did.

I wasn't used to being explored this much. He took his ship and sailed through me thoroughly. He pulled at my hair, knotting it into his fist. My neck practically popped when he pulled it back, but something within me, some little, devilish, devious, succubus, loved the frustrations he showed. He shoved himself inside of me without any sign of it happening. He groaned as he thrusted, and it was difficult to even breathe. The tension that had built up just melted around his thick cock as he thrusted over and over, pulling me into each, reaching deep inside my gut. He might have poked my stomach.

Mmm. I just couldn't help but tighten myself around him, giving him the great pleasures he was giving me. Making me hot. HOT. Wet. Too WET. Just dripping as he fucked me, clapping my ass against his thighs. I moaned in the sheets, muffled by the cotton-full pleasure that escaped my lips. He slid out of me, turned me onto my back, and threw my legs over his shoulders. He devoured me like a dinner plate, licking the juice away, tasting every ounce of cum. I leaked like a faucet. He slapped my face, but I accepted it. As excited as I was, getting a slap back that I had given him earlier, must've matched the pleasure he felt. I liked it and didn't know I would like such things, but he made me feel like a different woman.

He crawled over me, his thighs pressing my shoulders together, and his cock hung heavy against my nose, long between my eyes as he let my cum wet my face. I licked it, knowing it would turn him on even more. His girth flinched when I did, and the head of his cock rested against my pink lips. I warmed my mouth with a smack, then sucked him as hard as I could, practically trying to tug his cock off his body, wishing I could use my hands to jerk at the same time.

He filled my throat with his girth, but I didn't gag like the girl in the video. I accepted my fate, letting his rod jab against the back of my throat until I could practically feel it trying to escape the back of my neck. Tears filled my eyes, but when he saw that my makeup was starting to blind me, he stopped thrusting my throat and went inside me again. Thrusting his body against mine, keeping my arms bound beneath me, but my legs as high as the ceiling. He licked and sucked my toes as he fucked me. Massaging across my calves and up my thighs until the pool, we made of cum drizzled on his bedsheets.

I was finished...But he kept going.

He kept turning me over, onto my stomach, then my back, then wrapping my legs around his face, to sucking his cock, to lifting me in the air, to making me squat-ride him. Though my wrist bled, I loved the pain. I loved the pleasure, and just when I thought he would cum, I came on him again, melting around his shaft like a Popsicle in the hot sun, soothing my lips around his girth and squeezing tight as I did. I just couldn't hold it in any longer. His name. I moaned his name, and he groaned as he did, and the second I was finished cumming, he had just started filling me with his milk, throbbing inside of me, then resting himself on his back as I tried to find the strength to fall over onto my side, still bound by the cuffs, as he relaxed comfortably.

"Gracie," he finally said, with his breath taken away.

"Yes, chief."

"Call me Duke...You are...remarkable." The last of my breaths mustered a chuckle as my naked body laid before him, cum dripping out of me like running water.

"Thank you...Duke. You are too." The bondage wasn't as bad as I thought it would be, of course, I would have to explain the cuff marks to Angie. She'll lose her mind once I told her about this. He crawled over to the nightstand beside his bed and reached inside. Through half-closed eyes of sleep, I looked over and watched as he counted cash. More cash than my eyes had ever seen. He then rested the stack beside me which read $10,000. I couldn't grab the cash because of my bindings, but I smiled up at him, and he smiled back.

"Next time," I told him. "I host."

"Next time?" He asked.

"Oh yes, chief. Next time, no tip needed."

Three Is a Party

Chapter 1: 7-Day Trial

My phone beeped for the sixth time in the past hour. It was only 9 AM, and I barely had finished my first morning coffee at work. What do I do? What do I say to him? I mean, what haven't I already said that he doesn't get? It's over. I can't do this anymore. You cheat! Ugh! My first break-up since high school and just thinking about it makes me want to put my head through this computer screen and cry until my tears fry it. I took a deep breath, practically a sigh, and tried to focus on my work.

Fingers punched into the keyboards around me help. It made it harder to think about Justin.

Every time a thought crossed my mind, someone started crunching buttons into their laptop. The muffled crunches behind each cubicle managed to make their way around me. If my cubicle wasn't in the very center of the Benztine's Marketing floor, it would've been harder to purposely look for distractions.

Sally stood from her cubicle, holding herself up by the arms. She was barely tall enough to stand from the floor and look over into my cubicle. She always used her chair to do so. Her face bright as the bright red lipstick she always wore, and her floral dress sat softly against her bleach-blonde hair and model-like shoulders. She had a better sense of fashion than I did, and her marketing plans for the company were amazing.

"Moira, you're dragging your face again?" I slouched my face on purpose to keep her asking questions in hopes it would make me feel better. She was my best friend and always knew exactly what to say or do to make me feel comfortable. I placed my head against my keyboard, and eventually, the computer started to beep, thinking I was trying to activate the hotkeys. I held up my phone.

"Remind me to smash this with a hammer during my lunch break, please."

"Justin still pestering you?" She took my phone and unlocked it. I don't ever put up a fight to take it back. She can respond just as well as me. "Well, we should tell him to go fuck himself for what he did." I jolted back to life and scrambled for the phone. I managed to retake control and shook my head endlessly.

"No, we shouldn't. Just--let him vent...again."

She sighed. "Fine, I just can't take seeing you mope around like this. Every few seconds, all I hear on the other side of this wall is--" And she started to moan, groan, pout, and mope.

"I can mope," I whined. "I'm a big girl." And I mustered up a smile.

"Well, we can always try other alternatives to help you move on."

"Alternatives?" She was about to say something, but paused and glared over my shoulder.

"Max? What the fuck? Girl talk." He laughed to himself, then sat back down. "Jesus. Boys. So nosey. Anyway. Yes, we need to get you to move on."

"I'm not ready to see anybody."

"Well," and she smirked with an evil twinkle in her eye. Whenever I have seen that look, I knew she had cooked up some sort of concoction. "You need to step into the new age, cupcake. Try out one of the million dating apps that are out there. Everyone uses them."

"But you never get to really--" Sally cowered down from her seat a bit, and we watched as one of the floor managers walked by, eyed us, but kept it moving. I lowered my voice. "You never really get to know someone on there. They're just words on a screen."

"But." She held up one finger. "You can feel them out first. Read some profiles. Get acquainted if you'd like."

"Those profiles and pictures could all be lies."

"In which case, when you meet them, you run the other way. Listen, do whatever you need to do, but please, just swipe right and try, Moira. There's plenty of men out there." Her eyes then shifted over my shoulder. Curly-headed Max had stood up once more, holding a perverted grin across his lips. "Just hope and pray to God that whoever you come across isn't anything like Max." *That's for sure.*

After work that day, Sally gave me some dating apps to try out and left for her usual workout routine with her gym partner. Taking advice from Sally wasn't like taking advice from just anybody. She had plenty of dating experience, and unlike myself at the time, married and happy with someone we both grew up with through middle and high school. Blake Wellington. Prom Queen and King made the dream happen. I didn't have as much luck as they, but still, I was lucky to still have them both in my life.

As I waited for the A train back to Queens from Times Square, I tried to keep my phone closer to my face, to keep people from seeing me trying out dating apps. The thought of someone seeing it would make me feel naked or like I was watching porn. I'd have to burn their eyes for misunderstanding. The first app I tried led to many disappointments. Some of the guys were cute, and some were way too good to have actually been real. Some guys photos looked photoshopped with apps, while others, posed without a shirt, flexed their muscles and had profiles as dull as a book failing to take off after the first ten pages.

Other guys who seemed decent enough had great photos, but once I messaged them and they finally got back to me, they'd already ask to meet in person. I wasn't up for it, and when I did tell them where I stood relationship-wise, my excuse as to why I can't meet, they'd call me a bitch or tell me that I looked ugly. Crazy how men take rejection. They just-- can't.

When I finally uninstalled that app, I was almost at the train stop in Queens. I started the second of the three apps she suggested. With this one, the guys would contact the girls first, and only then could they spark conversation. I found this one to be much better because it meant whoever connected to me, actually wanted to get to know me. But of course, I could not have been any more wrong.

I've received many messages and photo comments of vulgar, sexual things men said they wanted to do to me. The messages overflowed my inbox that I thought it could not have been possible for a mailbox to contain all those messages. Needless to say, most of the messages had the same contents: a simple *"Hi,"* which told me how boring and unspontaneous they must be. A spam message of another dating site, or in other words, goddamn bots, or so-and-so wants to share media, and my curious self couldn't help but select to open and find a hairy, curved hotdog or pig in a blanket cover my phone screen.

Instant blockage.

After getting home and starting the next download on the third app, showering became difficult. I couldn't get Justin out of my head. The moment I did start to push him from my mind, my phone started buzzing. Without even peeking at the bathroom sink at my phone, I knew it had to be him.

:Hey, text me back. Been trying to talk to you. Want to say I'm sorry.:

For the thousandth time. I already knew that everything he had to say was going to be the same thing. I'm sorry. I love you. Etcetera. I dressed myself and curled myself under the sheets as Netflix played. The new app was a bit better than most, giving the ability to swipe right for like or left to pass. I listened to Sally, swiping right continuously, barely taking a glance at any of the pictures. After a few hours, half-asleep, some came back as matches. Some in which either reminded me of Justin by their looks, or the types of guys you wouldn't want to walk past without gripping your purse tighter. There was one; however, that sent a beautiful message, speaking about my short, black hair, and blue eyes, and the freckles that rested beneath my eyes and across the bridge of my nose.

We talked for a while, and the conversation seemed great, but then, the way he spoke started to change. He started to get back to my looks, talking about one of the photos I posted when I was lying on my bed in my gown. He asked if he can see beneath them. I immediately knew he was like the rest, the only difference was, he knew the game better than most. He knew how to lead a girl on, and before his patience ran thin, he couldn't contain his ultimate goal long enough for me to see the real him.

I didn't bother deleting messages and blocking anymore. I just uninstalled. My hope for dating apps was over, yet I still clung onto the idea that maybe I was going about things the wrong way. Lucky enough for me, I had the perfect guy friend to give me his take.

"It's been a while since I've seen you, Moira," Blake said as he took a seat across from me. "Inviting me to this coffee shop in the middle of lunch hour. Doesn't quite sound like some casual catch-up."

"Because it isn't," I said, cupping my hands around my mug. "I know you and Sally have been through quite a bit since school, but you two found your way back to each other. Back to love. I'm just--" I sighed and looked around, hoping no one like Max from work was listening to this sob story.

"Just what?" I always loved how Blake's eyes gleaned when he was curious. Every girl throughout middle and high school had eyes for him, including me. Of course, Sally knew I did, eventually, but she never condemned me for it. She took it as a compliment. "Moira? You're just what?"

"I'm just desperate to find someone. To settle down how you and Sally have. I know that sounds ridiculous. To envy something your friends have and--"

"No, no." He smiled. "It's not ridiculous at all. Moira, listen, Sally and I have broken up more times than I can count before we were able to finally make this work. That might be the same for you and Justin."

"No." I shook my head then took a sip, almost choking on it just from the thought of being back with Justin again. I missed him, but he wasn't good for me, and as many times as I had been told I could have done better, I've finally been able to make friends with those terms. "Me and Justin are over."

"Well, what have you been doing to move on?"

"Listening to Sally." He almost laughed out loud.

"That sounds promising. Love my wife to death, but sometimes her advice can be a bit misleading than what you actually need. What'd she have you do? Spend a ton of money on clothes, shopping, and spoiling yourself?"

"I haven't tried that, but that doesn't sound too bad of an idea," I laughed. "But no, she had me try dating apps."

"Dating apps," he scoffed and sipped his coffee. "Those things are cancerous."

"What should I do? Any suggestions?"

"Yeah, actually. You're going on dating apps, hoping to find love. Well, the way it sounds right now, you're still healing from what happened between you and Justin. Maybe love isn't something you should be looking for right now."

"Are you going to say I need to work on myself, create a better me for the next person, blah, blah, blah?"

"Not at all, actually. I was going to say, and don't take this the wrong way, but I was going to say maybe instead of looking for love you look for--" And he paused for me to fill in the blanks.

"Sex." Didn't take long. He nodded.

"Hook-up apps."

"Yeah, me on a hook-up site would go really well. I could've just taken my pick from the lot I seen on the apps I uninstalled." He dug into his pocket and removed a pen and paper. I suppose I should've been open-minded talking to an established author. They're full of ideas. Questionable ones might I add.

"Check out these two." He placed the paper in front of me, then clocked his watch. "I should get going." I tucked the slip into my pocket, wondering if these are the apps he used while he and Sally were cheating on each other.

"Yeah, same. Meeting up with Sally."

"Kiss her for me," he said, as he rose from his chair.

"Will do."

Chapter 2: The Scale

Sally curled herself around my arm. Times Square buzzed from car horns, people yelling through cell phones, music and ads playing on big screens, and people selling their businesses every city block we walked. I kissed her cheek, and she smiled like a child.

"That was from Blake," I told her.

"Ugh! Love my tiger. How'd the meet-up go with him? Give you any advice I couldn't?"

"He told me to stop looking for Justin in these dating apps and to hookup with someone."

"Hmm, usually, I don't like his ideas no matter how much of a creative genius he believes he is, but that's an idea I can't seem to find a rebuttal for."

"The both of you, I swear. Meant for each other."

"You need new tastes. I mean, come on. Maybe you just need to fuck Justin out of you, and that'll get you to move on."

"What?" I laughed. "You can't just fuck someone out of you."

"Oh, yes. You can. Believe me." She put more pep in our steps, I could practically hear her heels clicking on the sidewalk as we walked. "Take a look around, Moira." I listened, staring at pigeons, who zig-zagged their way between ankles. A rat might have fell into the sewer. The buzz all around me made it hard to focus in general. "What do you see?"

I was going to say birds, rats, and pollution, but instead, I thought of something deep.

"Opportunity."

"You're cute," she said. "Not exactly what I was looking for, but yes, actually. Opportunity. You have the opportunity to take your pick from the lot now that you are a free agent and take someone home." It sounded repelling. "You see all these men? Look at them. We got this guy here. Gray suit, matching pants, white shirt, black tie, well-tamed black hair. His face just practically says Christian Grey." He was handsome, but no.

"I'm not into torture."

"How about that guy?" She nodded at a man wearing a plain, white t-shirt, denim jeans with a few stylish rips, and short brown hair. "What would you rate him on a scale of 1 to Channing Tatum?" I smiled, and the man even nodded at us. Sally winked.

"Definitely Channing Tatum," I told her.

"Oh, how about him? I love my chocolate with wine now and then. Shaved head. Those man boobs poking right through that button up. On a scale of 1 to Morris Chestnut?"

No contest. "Morris Chestnut."

"See? You don't have much of a type, Moira. New York is full of many great things, and one of those things? Mouth-watering men. They're everywhere." Of all the men we passed, it did seem almost every man in Times Square was someone I either wish I knew, slept with during my college days, or at least was a gay best friend just to have the excuse of walking around with him. Sally then paused a moment on the sidewalk and bit her lips.

"That man," she said, staring past me. I glanced at the direction we were walking after having her trail behind. She didn't need to break down his appearance. This man was a walking dessert. Chiseled, tan face, light-brown eyes, that gym has been doing him right. Had to be straight out of one of those Amazonian movies. A warrior, long, black pony-tail down his back. Could practically see his abs poking through his black v-neck t-shirt. "He's the one." She said.

"He's the what?" Sally nudged me as he walked by, and as much as of a klutz I was, I fell right into those arms. He caught me and I stiffened up, straight as a pole, almost hitting the ground. His arms pulled me back up as straight as a pencil, and I couldn't lift my jaw.

"Are you alright, miss?" I was paralyzed. Sally hopped a few times to see me over his broad shoulders, mouthing for me to talk. I just couldn't stop staring at him.

"I'm fine. Nice...catch." He smiled, and my God, his father must be a dentist.

"It was nothing."

"Sorry I bumped into you."

"No harm done." Sally kept ushering for me to keep conversation going, but I already felt it ending. "Well, it was nice bumping into you."

"Moira," I mustered.

"Moira." He smiled again. "Enjoy your afternoon, Moira." He started to walk off, and Sally hopped up and down, angrily in her heels, and I mouthed for her to help me.

"Ask him out," she hissed. "Ask him out." I couldn't think. He was walking back the other way now. I'd have to call for him, but I didn't know his name.

"Ummm...Uhhh," I stammered, bringing my hand to my head. "Ex-Excuse me. Excuse me!" It grabbed his attention and plenty of others as well. He pivoted in place but didn't come back over. "I--" It felt like I was about to give some Shakespearean monologue. I had an entire audience. Typical New York City. "I have a little time left from lunch. Want to, uhh, join me?" New Yorkers looked at him, and he nodded.

"Sure. I have some time." I turned back to Sally, and her eyes were as big as watermelons. *What?!* I mouthed. *Text me!* She mouthed back, and she hurried ahead, looking back every few seconds as me and this stranger walked together.

"Moira, right?" he asked.

"Yeah. You?"

"Samson."

"Samson?" I asked, almost putting a stop to our pace. "That's quite a strong name."

"I'd like to think of myself as a strong guy. So, tell me about yourself?" I got into my marketing job with Sally, my childhood home, college, and other random things, but made sure to keep the topic as far away from Justin and the break-up as possible. He told me about how he's only in town for a couple more weeks, and it was sort of a downer. I was fine with it, though, being that the objective wasn't to fall in love with this guy but sleep with him. Even that seemed like an impossible task, yet so did asking him to walk with me so, must've been something he saw in, or on me, that he liked.

After work, he invited me out to a steak dinner. I'm a vegetarian, but I wasn't going to be a party pooper at the same time. He apologized for the choice of the restaurant even, but they had alfredo and garlic bread, which was more than enough for my petite self to eat. He talked about the company he owns, how he travels and manages a blog. He's one of those Go Green kinds of folk. The perfect things you didn't think you can find in just one man was all bunched within him. When he invited me over after dessert, I was hesitant, knowing that I just met him and how the last guy seemed perfect until he told me what he really wanted. But then I figured if Samson just really wanted me in bed, then I would have fulfilled my mission as well. So I accepted.

We got to his place, and he seemed like a different Samson than the one on met on the street. He couldn't keep his eyes, and specifically, his hands off of me. He lusted for me, kissing hungrily into my neck before I could even remove my shirt. The roles switched when he took off his shift. This warrior's pack was stacked in an eight-pack, his chest as heavy as a gorilla's as it jiggled when he flexed them for me. I wrapped myself around him, hugged and caressed his back, and he sucked on my earlobes. The moment he laid me down, I kept thinking, this is it. This is where I can finally fuck Justin out of me, and Samsom was going to do me and do me well.

But I was wrong.

All of that foreplay and teasing ended abruptly when he got inside. I gave him one good squeeze of my vaginal muscles, and he practically busted his nut and even had tears flowing from his eyes. I asked what he was crying for and he said, "This is the first time I've slept with someone since my ex-fiance."

The man was just as broken as I was. Two balls of emotional Jell-O, tossing and turning in sheets together, is never a good idea. When he fell asleep atop of me, he weighed an elephant. I managed to reach my phone on the nightstand, pulling it over to me by the tips of my fingers since I could barely move. I messaged Sally.

:*How'd it go?*:

:*Terrible.*:

:*Seriously? That guy was a hunk. What did you do to him?*:

:Nothing. He's as broken as me.:

:Ohhhh, shit. That sucks. You need to get out of there.:

:Oh I will, but I guess that won't be until he wakes up.:

Chapter 3: One Last Attempt

The greatest thing I did the next morning was block his number. Not that I wanted to, per se, but I only thought I should because now I was having TWO men messaging me, apologizing for what they did, or was not able to do which was at least help me finish. The more I typed and focused on my work, the easier things went, at least until Sally started poking her head over my cubicle.

"A crybaby? Seriously?"

"Tell me about it. This is your fault," I joked.

"My fault. Listen, I thought I was doing you a favor."

"Quite the opposite." I shook my head and sighed. "I give up, you know. I've tried these apps, and they're almost as bad as just going out and meeting people in person. Hooking up with guys. Not what I do."

"Well, I do have one last suggestion." Max stood from his cubicle, smiling ear to ear. We stared at him, and his smile faded. He sat back down.

"I'm not sure I'd even want to hear this suggestion. I've already taken one from both you, and Blake and it got me into the bed with a man-baby."

"Aren't all men babies? Anyway, check this out." She took my phone, as usual, and began typing. She handed the phone back, and it was downloading an app.

"What's this?"

"Something I've heard about some time ago. I've even tried to use it once, but it's been a while."

"Escort service?"

"Mhmm."

"No," I shook my head and immediately deleted it. "I'm not into that."

"Well, I don't know what else you want me to say. I've tried."

"Perhaps I can help," Max said. We didn't realize he had made his way over. "Hi, Moira."

"Max," Sally said. "What advice could you possibly give her?"

"Well, Sally," he said with annoyance in his voice, "I just so happen to be leaving this company next week to continue running my business full-time. I've had plenty of success, and no longer need to be here."

"Business," Sally almost laughed. "What business?"

"This," he said, as he navigated into his phone. He showed his home screen and pointed at an app. "The best app to help you move on."

"You've made an app?" Sally said with a drag. "Seriously?"

"We've generated enough money to buy this floor of its employees so tread carefully. You might be working for me one day."

"Keep dreaming."

"What's your app all about?" I asked him.

"You can't possibly be considering taking advice from Max, the creep."

"Moira, you've tried finding love again. Failed. Justin is still anal raping you via text. And you've tried to hook up with someone, yet that led to what you both called...a man-baby?"

"Lack for a better description yet accurate." I shrugged.

"This app gets rid of those failures. No need to look for love, and no need to just hook up with someone who just may be going through what you are with your ex."

"Okay, I think you're marketing a bit too much now, red-head," Sally said. "Get to the point. What's this app?"

"It's called Three'sa Party."

"What?" I asked.

"Three...is...a...party. It's a 3-some app that has couples who are looking for people like you to have fun with. Not just hooking up, but think of yourself as being happy with being the third wheel. Of course, it is usually just for hook-ups, but we have data that proves that some form long-term relationships with the couple they've met."

"So, it's a hook-up app for a threesome?" I asked. "Just to clarify." He shrugged.

"Lack for a better explanation. Yes." I looked over at Sally, and she was typing into her phone.

"What are you doing?"

"Seeing how legit it is, of course."

"Well, I won't take any more of your time, ladies. Give my app a try, Moira. 99% satisfaction guaranteed." Chances are, with my luck, that 1% was going to happen.

When I got home that evening, I had a dinner date with Max's new app. I sat at the kitchen island, forking through a bowl of spaghetti as I scanned over couple profiles. I hadn't finished completing mine. I figured what was the point in bothering with setting up all my info and posting a profile picture if there was a strong chance I was going to uninstall the app before bedtime anyway?

Most of the profiles I came across were definitely looking for a third person for some fun. Some were open to experimentation, and others were interested in long-term relationships. I didn't know this was an actual thing. To share *someone* with someone *else*. There were couples of all sorts. Those who were into BDSM, sex slave, and other peculiar, sexual pleasures. Those who were part of the LGBTQ-RSTUVWXYZ--or however many sexual orientations and identities there are now--

community. Too many choices, I didn't know where to start.

But then I came across them.

Another private profile of a couple interested in showing the ropes of this new form of sexual orientation of Three'sa Party. It might have been the best place to start for someone like me. They didn't have much of a bio, only that they are quite experienced with this sort of thing, and the right individual interested wouldn't participate in anything they weren't comfortable with.

I opened a new message box to inbox them. Wasn't sure exactly where or how to start. Do I tell them about myself? Do I just say hello and hope it opens up conversation? Do I tell them I'm new to this and they'll take it from there? I finished my dinner, still trying to figure out what message would get them to respond.

In trying to find the courage to message them, I was going to need some help. Not Sally's. Not Max's. Not Blake's. Sure as hell not Justin's. This sort of thing needed liquid courage. This decision to conjure up a confident message required alcohol.

I poured wine. Red. Get myself nice and as buzzed as a bumblebee. I walked circles around the kitchen island, wine glass between my fingers, phone and open message in my other hand. When my eyes began to feel hazy and lips began to quiver into smirks, I sat back down in the stool and typed.

:As inexperienced as this slender Brunette is in this nightgown, gushing over herself with a glass of wine in hand, how might someone like myself interest an

experienced couple as yourselves? Open for business? Make me your customer.:

Before even reading it to myself, I sent it and almost immediately wondered what the hell was I thinking. I pressed my forehead against the island, and moments later, my phone buzzed. A notification from the app. When I opened it, it was them. I thought they would send a manual to me on what would happen next, but instead, they only responded with four words.

:When are you available?:

Chapter 4: The Meeting

The Uber dropped me off to a wide, two-floor, white house with cream curtains in the windows. Candles rested in each window and gave a golden glow. I've seen this house before. A while ago. That black bar fence. The red door with a golden bell.

The Christmas party. It was the last time I had seen this house. Many of my co-workers were there. Max was the life of the party. What were the chances he and some partner of his were inviting me to his house? The thought was disgusting, and my Uber had just left. But it all made sense. Max was the one who sent the invitations out to everyone for the party. I don't remember who he was hosting with, but his name was on the email, and he did the decorations as well. I knew the pervert must've been making his move with me. I at least thought he always had the hots for Sally apart from how much they fought. To Max, it was flirtation.

I turned back to the street and navigated through the Uber app, hoping I'd be able to catch my driver to send a message. But the moment I got to the screen, I heard the front door of the house open. I kept myself grounded, where I stood until I heard a voice I recognized.

"Hey. Are you Brunette87?" It wasn't Max's voice. I turned the door, and there she stood, shock spreading across her face. "Moira?"

"Sally?" I approached the front door, and her look of confusion turned into amusement.

"How is--"

"This possible?" I finished, trying to force myself to smile.

"More like--embarrassing," she said.

"Is it her?" Another voice asked, and a few seconds later, Blake joined her, and his face flushed. "Oh, hi, Moira. We weren't expecting you." He looked at Sally. "We were just going to--"

"Actually," and Sally turned to him. "We were expecting her." He looked confused for a moment, then Sally nodded, and his eyes widened.

"Well, that's quite a surprise."

"Would you like to come in?" Sally asked. I looked down the

street, and my phone buzzed from low battery.

"I guess it wouldn't hurt." They stepped out of the way, and Blake took my jacket as Sally closed the door.

We chatted at their dining room table with lots of wine. It was only building on what I had already drank, and both Sally and Blake's eyes were starting to look like glass. We joked about work, and Blake told us about his new erotica work in progress. When the conversation started to die and things began to get a little quiet, I took notice how much Sally kept adjusting the straps on her nightgown.

"It's pretty warm in here. Isn't it?"

"Yeah," Sally responded, almost eating the last word from his mouth. Blake removed his shirt, and his jock like body wasn't anything he had as a book nerd through middle and high school, and other women would've thought he was that popular high school quarterback. They started staring at me in silence off and on, and each time I looked up from my lap, I felt as if I was supposed to do something.

"I know how awkward this seems," Sally finally said. She rose from her chair and joined my lap. She wrapped her arms around my neck, and her breath lingered of the sweet, pink Moscato she practically finished on her own. "But look at it this way, Moira. We won't force you to do anything you wouldn't want us to. You can just-- leave if you feel uncomfortable."

"Or, you could stay," Blake added, and Sally smirked at him. When she turned back to me, her lips were much closer to mine than before as she spoke. I could almost taste her next words as she said them.

"Would this help you decide?" She pressed her lips against mine, and the tip of her tongue parted between them. We folded and massaged tongues as heat built up my arms, into my chest, and boiled into my face. As long as I've known Sally, I never thought it would be possible she'd make me feel this--sensation. Attracted to her. She held the back of my head with her hand, guiding the pace, sucking my tongue into her mouth, then resting her hand between my warm thighs. When our lips separated, she stared into my pupils, and the corners of her mouth curled up and Blake's did the same.

I forgot how to breathe. I couldn't turn my gaze from her eyes and was so paralyzed beneath her that I hadn't realize Blake was standing over the both of us, waiting for my answer.

"I liked that," I told her.

"There's more of it where it came from. Would you like to see?" I couldn't answer. Blake lifted my face by the chin and didn't give me much a choice when he started tonguing into my throat. He always made me hot, giving me all these thoughts I shouldn't have about my friend's husband. But those feelings were there. I wanted him. I wanted to fuck him. I wanted to fuck Sally, which is what I only learned in the time it took for her to kiss me. I only nodded because I couldn't speak. They smiled at each other, and they both took me by the hand and led me upstairs to their bedroom.

We were naked in fuschia sheets, folding into each other's limbs as we kissed, fingered, and handjobbed Blake's thick shaft. They lied me bare onto my back. Blake kept his head between my legs as Sally became my pillow, holding my legs back by the ankles. Blake's tongue devoured every inch inside of me, slithering its way around like a mindless snake, and each breath he took tickled my clit. He sucked on it, pulling and tugging with his lips, making it erect in his warm, wet mouth. I couldn't keep from shaking.

Sally played with my nipples and squeezed my breasts as she squatted just above my face for me to eat her as they played me like an instrument. My toes curled and clinched. Blake just wouldn't stop.

His groans and nibbling slowed down as he sensually parted my pussy lips with his fingers and stuck his tongue back inside me. I let out a moan, but Sally sat down, muffling my moans with her pussy in my mouth, making me lick the wetness between the lips.

"Turn over," Blake ordered, and Sally got off and laid back against the headboard. She grabbed onto my head and made me eat her furiously as Blake shoved himself full inside of me from behind. He pushed down on my lower back, making me arch, then pulled me into each thrust as Sally moaned and grinded her pussy against my mouth.

"Yes, Moira. Eat that kitty." She licked her lips and tossed her head back, and I tried gripping around Blake tighter, but he thrusted harder, clapping my cheeks against his lap, grunting like an animal. I never knew how much he might have wanted me all this time, but it was showing.

"Sally. Bend over on top of her." Blake was giving orders like a commander. Sally didn't contest or say a word. She arched herself over me, both of our asses facing Blake, leaving us vulnerable for whatever he wanted to do. He pulled out of me, shoved himself inside of Sally, and when I heard her moan, I rested my face into the pillow, keeping my back arched until Blake shoved inside of me again. Then into Sally. Then into me, mixing our love juices with each other. When he stopped, he ate us both, working from our vagina to our asses and again.

He threw Sally off of me, then pulled my face towards his dick and shoved it into my mouth.

I wasn't ready at all, for the force he thundered into the back of my throat should've made me gag, yet I didn't realize I didn't have a gag reflex. He threw me back down onto my back.

"I'm going to finish on her," he told Sally, and she smiled and nodded.

"I'll help you, baby."

They put me back onto my back, and Sally placed her head on my lower abdomen. She watched as Blake tickled my clit with the tip of his cock, and each time it flicked, I shivered and shook. I held Sally's head full of gold hair, and Blake's abs tumbled atop each other as he leaned forward to shove himself inside of me. He gasped as he did, but it was easy for him to slip right in. I squeezed and held onto his cock tight to help him. Sally even loosely gripped around his cock with her hand as he thrusted. He had the best of both worlds. Penetration and handjob at the same time.

Before he could moan once and toss his head back, I was already milking around his cock, cumming, but grinding against him, feeling the heat build and boil more in my face as Sally rooted for him to bust his load on me. When he threw himself back and gripped his cock in his hand, Sally and I had the same thought to taste his warm gift.

We bent over on the bed, mouths wide open, tongues sticking out, and holding onto his waist as he jerked himself over us. Then, he shot his cum onto our faces, and it dripped on our mouths. We licked and kissed each other, swapping what we caught with our tongues as he then let us suck his cock a bit to drain what might have been left inside of him.

The next morning, we had breakfast in silence but smiled. When I finished, we still hadn't said a word to each other, but the attraction from last night had remained. Sally led me to the door, and she sighed in delight, and I did the same as my Uber driver pulled up.

"That was something," I told her. She nodded.

"It was. You better make sure you get some rest this weekend."

"You too," I said, referring to them both. Blake nodded and smiled. "I'll see you Monday?" Sally shook her head.

"Actually, I was hoping we'd see you again this weekend. This time, we take a trip to the mountains in Bristol. There's a cabin and snow up there. It'd be fun."

"I'd love to."

"Good," she said. "So get the rest you need. We want you to come with the same energy you had last night."

The More the Merrier

Chapter 1: The Invitation

I never agreed to this, yet here I am, packing all this stuff to see friends who haven't mattered in over a decade. Who throws a part out in the middle of nowhere just to catch-up? We could've met at a coffee shop, or I don't know, anywhere, but the middle of the woods? The front door opened, and Bryson came in from work dressed in his suit coat and tie, briefcase in his hand. He hurried to the bedroom and kissed my cheek as I continue to pack.

"Hey, baby? Almost ready? We gotta leave soon."

"I guess." I threw a pair of panties inside the travel bag, and he sighed.

"Why are you still upset about going? I told you it was going to be fun, I promise."

"We haven't seen any of these guys since we graduated from high school, and now, we're going to spend a weekend with them in the middle of the woods in some cabin?" I tossed more clothes into the bag, not caring about folding them.

"You're worried something bad is going to happen? Who do you think these people are? Murderers or something? That movie Get Out really got to your head, huh?" He smirked, and I found myself raising my fist.

"It's not funny. I'm being serious. We don't know these people anymore. A lot could happen and can change a person in ten years. Besides, we just had the class reunion months ago."

"And we weren't there because YOU didn't want to go. That's probably why they invited us to this party. To catch up." I shook my head and headed into the bathroom for the rest of my things. I reached into the bathroom cabinet for my medication, and when I closed the mirror, Jacob was there. He put his face and dreads against my cheek and curled his arms around me.

"Stop worrying," he said into my ear. He moved my black curls from my cheek and kissed into my neck. "I'll be right there, and if we don't like the presentation, then we'll leave early. Simple as that." I sighed. He always found ways to still get me to do things I don't want to do. I also did the same to him.

"Fine. Not a second later, either."

"Simone, Simone. Not a second later." I took my depressants with a cup of water as Jacob headed back into the room. I scanned at the invitation pinned into the mirror's crease. They obviously had some kind of money to have this kind of red clay seal that reminded me of those Harry Potter letters. I flipped it open, and there's only but a sentence long of the invitation. Everything else on the card was blank. No decorations or stamps or pictures or graphics. Nothing.

"You have been invited to our manor for a presentation." It was simple. Straight to the point without any clue as to what presentation and who else was going. What was even more disturbing were the ones who sent the invitation. Michael and his "butler."

"You must know something about this." I heard our bags close and zip, and he wheeled them past the bathroom door.

"I do, but there's no way I'm telling you what it's about. I'll just say I know you'll love it." That didn't help much. It could be anything, but since we were officially going, I might as well make the best of it.

We traveled up high hills, leaving Seattle behind us in the rain. Jacob kept the music going, and he made for damn sure I would hear his voice over the artist's. He kept looking over, trying to get me to sing, but all I could think about was the party. How many people would be going? Is it just another pyramid scheme? I hoped not, knowing the last time

I've been invited to some party presentation, our friends were trying to get us to buy into some $500 business, and we'd get paid as we recruited more and could use some point system to travel. It was all about building residual income. I can't sit through another one of those. He tapped my knee with his hand.

"We're almost there."

"This isn't another pyramid scheme, is it?"

"No, Simone. We've tried that already, remember? I didn't last a month, and you didn't even start."

"Yes, which means I made a good call...And I almost feel like I'm doing the same thing now."

"I promise you'll be smiling before the weekend is out." He smiled and looked over and seemed so sure of himself. I loved him for that though. It's the most attractive thing about him. His persistence. I've decided if I was going to be spending the weekend there, then I might as well make friends with the idea. At least try to make friends.

After a while of driving, the road turned to dirt, and there were more trees around us than I had ever seen before. We followed the path, driving through the rain with the high beams, and I could've sworn that, at any moment, a deer was going to hop out from the woods and make us crash. The path started to incline, forming its way up into the sky that seemed like it could last forever. Moreover, the city was far away, but we could see it in the distance, down below. Once we parted from the trees, the path coiled itself out of the woods, and before us stood a tall and wide, white mansion with many glass windows and doors, blue lights, and torches on the balcony.

"Whoa," Jacob said as he pulled up the path. "This place is unbelievable."

"Maybe they stuck with the pyramid," I said, but he was right. It was beautiful, and their plants were even sculpted into different animals. They had fountains and statues in their vineyard of luscious flowers resting inside of a small greenhouse next to a garage that fit six cars already.

"We're not the only ones here," I said.

"Of course not."

"Do I know any of these people?"

"Let's assume you do, would it change how you feel about all this?"

"Not one bit."

"Didn't think so." He pulled the car up beside the others in the last vacant spot. When we got out of the car, I heard a voice coming from the house, which sounded like someone had been singing. As they approached, we took our bags from the trunk and he stepped into the light.

"Mike!" Jacob exclaimed, almost dropping the bags.

"Jake!" He outstretched his arms, and they folded around each other. "So great to see you, man! You look great! Longer hair, but still looking like you can put on a helmet and pads." He patted Jacob's back then gave him a squeeze at the shoulders.

"You look great too, man!" And Jacob did the same to him. "Not any bigger than I remember."

"Well, you haven't seen other parts of me to confirm that!" And they pointed at each other and laughed hysterically. Boys and their sexual jokes. "That is not Simone!" I peered around Jacob and I gave Mike a slight wave and smile. He stepped away from Jacob, dressed in a fine, dark-blue suit and black tie, and his hair was slicked back and clung to the back of his neck. He looked like he belonged in a 1920s movie like Gatsby, but it looked great on him. I was actually impressed.

"Wow, um, Mike, you look good too." And he threw his arms around me and squeezed tighter than I wanted. His hands caressed across my back as he hugged and breathed. I practically felt his heart pounding through his wet suit. When he finally released me, he held me out in front of him, and I grimaced as his eyes ran me up and down.

"Mike, you really shouldn't be out here in that nice suit," Jacob said.

"You're right. Let me help with the bags." He took mine from my hand, and before Jacob could tell him otherwise, he took Jacob's in the other. "Follow me." I rolled my eyes as he led the way and Jacob shrugged. We followed him up the path, sheltering ourselves from the rain with haste. When we got up the million steps that lighted each step we took, he placed the bags down before the door and had to use both hands to push it open.

I felt I walked into some expensive hotel. He stutter-stepped inside as he took the bags. The golden chandeliers hung high above in rows and columns, and their jewels shined like diamonds. A statue of a merman, wielding a trident in his hand, rested in the center of the marble-floored room. It took a while to realize that the merman was Mike himself. Momentarily, an old man dressed in a black suit and tie and cloth over his forearm came down the steps. He bowed to us, and we smiled and bowed back.

"I'll take these upstairs," he said, with a yawn in his voice.

"Thank you, Malfus," Mike said. "Shall we?"

As Malfus took our luggage up the marble steps, Mike led the way down long hallways, talking to Jacob about the places he had traveled, the places he plans to see, and how excited he was to have us there. I couldn't keep my eyes off the place itself. Their talk became nothing but indistinct chatter. These walls. Almost each had a different painting on them of naked men and women, most in which the settings took place in the woods while others were naked with their friends having a cup of tea. This couldn't have possibly been the same Mike who came to school with disheveled hair, barely done his homework and spent most of his time all senior year just focusing on the senior prank. This was a different man. A successful man. A man who loved to touch and smile and certainly loved nakedness. Voices started to come from another hallway when we reach an intersection.

"Who's all here?" I asked him, finally finding my chance.

"People you'll be happy to see." He approached two large doors and stopped before them. A smile spread across his lips, and his teeth gleaned in the light like some pearly vampire. "I can't wait until we have some fun. You're going to love it, especially you, Simone." His freakish smile feasted on me and Jacob smiled too. Something was odd about Mike apart from all his success. When he pushed the doors open, I, at least, saw we had something in common though.

Chapter 2: Scheme

Friends. The other guests were others I hadn't seen since school, but they were my close friends, and it almost felt as if we've never been apart. Buck and Kim been together forever. I've always thought since they were kids, they were meant to be. Buck played on the football team with Jacob, and I was a cheerleader with Kim, but our friendship went past sports. We've traveled places together before college and even visited each other during our freshman year. Kim always loved her black men, and Buck always loved his Asians.

Tim and Hannah, I had believed to be broken up just weeks before graduation, but seeing how they are now, curled up together on the white sofa before a table of liquor bottles, they seemed to be having the time of their lives. Last I heard, Tim had moved to Arizona. Must've traveled all this way with Hannah. Hannah, I remembered to be a blonde, but this woman now had jet black hair, even cut short to the collarbone. Last and certainly not least, the one who I least expected being there was Nikki. My BFF.

"Simone! Jacob!" Buck exclaimed, rising from his seat, choking a beer by the neck of the bottle.

"What's going on, Buck!" Jacob exclaimed. "Damn, brodie, I haven't seen you in a while. Didn't you play college football for Rutgers."

"He did," Kim said, standing and giving us hugs. "Until he hurt that leg of his."

"Jacob. Simone," Tim said, and he smirked and held up his glass. Hannah did the same. "If we didn't hear you two were coming, we would not have been here."

"Really?" I said, thinking he might have been exaggerating.

"Oh, yes, indeed," Tim said. "Hannah couldn't stop talking about you coming since we've heard. Certainly giving me quite an earful."

"Now he's exaggerating," Hannah said. "Don't let him fool you. Tim is still a raging alcoholic, so we know why he's here."

"The drinks," we all said and started laughing.

"Going to say hi to me yet?" Nikki rose from a second white couch, wine glass between her fingers. She was much more beautiful than I remembered. Fit. Slender. Long, dark brown hair. Chestnut skin that practically glowed in her wine-colored dress. She might have gone on and became a model as she used to joke about.

"Nikki," I said, almost unable to even say her name. "Pleasant surprise."

"When I heard my runaway-for-love BFF was coming to the party, I didn't believe it. So, I flew out here to see for myself."

"And, are you disappointed?"

She shook her head. "Not in the slightest. You look good." And her eyes scanned over me. "Better than what I remembered."

"I can say the same for you." As we spoke, everyone else remained quiet. Tim held a grin on his face and sighed.

"You two should get a room," he said, then took another sip from his drink. "It's not like there aren't thirty or so to choose from."

"Jesus, Tim," Jacob laughed and shook his head. "You find entertainment everywhere."

"I find the best entertainment in a glass."

"Alright," Mike said, clasping his hands together. Nikki's eyes never left me, and it was difficult keeping eye contact with her. Something about her was different. Not in a bad way, but better. Same as everyone else. I felt they were the same people I remembered, but then I also felt a huge part of them was different. One thing's for sure, I don't ever remember Nikki giving me such eyes. I felt like a meal to her, waiting to be eaten. "If you all would kindly have a seat, we'll get started shortly, I promise." We listened, and Malfus returned and stood by patiently.

I sat beneath Jacob's arm on a third white couch that also faced the central floor. The living room was massive. It probably shouldn't be called a living room. Nikki's eyes still had yet to leave me, and when they finally did, she stretched herself out on the couch.

"Nikki and I have been doing this program for what? Six years now?" He asked her, and she nodded. "And we felt this was something we needed to share with you, Simone."

"Just me?" I asked, confused. "What? Everyone else

knows what all this is about?" They nodded.

"Pretty much, homegirl," Tim said and smiled.

"It's an hour-long presentation, so if anyone would like to use the restroom now, it's back near the front doors and up the stairs. First door you'll see on the right." I raised my hand and rose.

"If we're having some pyramid thing or secret cult service soon, I'll go now." I headed back to the front door area and up the steps. I still couldn't believe Mike was able to afford a place like this. Pyramid scheme or something else, I couldn't deny where I was, nor could I deny how much the others seemed to be doing well also. When I found the bathroom, the door was made of glass, and the lining was made of gold. I thought someone might have been able to see through it, but when I went to flicked the light switch, it turned the tint of the glass to black. You could only see outside of it, but in.

I fixed my hair, brightened a bit of makeup over the bags under my eyes, and spent some time looking in the mirror at myself, wondering if I might have strengthened my argument against Jacob, would I still be home. After a while, I decided to face it all. I hit the switch to the bathroom glass and found Nikki standing there. She had the same look on her face from earlier.

"Nikki, you scared the hell out of me."

"I'm sorry." She smiled and played with the end of one of my curls.

"Have to use it?"

"No. Just wanted to see you. It's been a while."

"Yeah, I know. Haven't seen you in years."

"I didn't mean that."

"Then what did you mean?" Down the hall, a moan crept from one of the rooms. I frowned a bit, wondering if the kind of moan I heard was the moan of fucking. Nikki didn't seem to pay it any attention. She only glanced down the hallway, then shook her head. "You heard that too, right?"

She nodded. "Yeah. What about it?" What did she mean, "What about it?" Was she not curious? I walked past her and down the hall towards one of the rooms. All of them were closed, but one was cracked open. Barely a speck of light came out of it. Nikki followed close behind me, and when I peeked through the crack, some guy was shoving himself into a much smaller brunette as she bent over before him and moaned into a white bed sheet. She bit the corner of the pillow and it stretched from her teeth as she tossed her head back. The man grabbed a handful of her hair and yanked her into each thrust as her ass just clapped against him like a drum. Nikki reached in front of me and closed the door.

"We shouldn't be up here disturbing their session."

"Session? You mean their fucking?"

"If that's what you saw." She smirked and shook her head.

"What the hell do you call that?" I asked, trying not to laugh. I thought she might have been joking, but her smile faded.

"Exactly what I said it was." She took me by the hand and led me back down the stairs and to the living room.

"Needed an escort?" Jacob asked when he saw Nikki bringing me in.

"No."

"I just wanted to make sure she didn't get lost." She released me, and we both took our places back. "You can start the presentation," she told Mike.

"Yes, yes, please," Buck said.

"So we can get to the fun already," Tim said, taking yet another sip from his glass. Mike grabbed a remote from the fireplace then clicked a couple buttons. A large screen, larger than two men could possibly carry themselves, rose from the marble floor. When it settled in place, he powered it on, and I saw Tim rocking back and forth in his seat with excitement. He clapped his hand against his glass, an applause which clinked from his wedding ring.

"Now, my friends," Mike said. "You'll see how this has given us the life we've always wanted to live."

Chapter 3: Presentation Is Everything

The video's actors and actresses were as terrible and as a porno movie. The melodramatic tone of voice. Their word choice and diction. The corniness of how they responded to the purpose of their "surprise" visit. I certainly didn't get any pyramid scheme vibes. I had gotten something completely different.

The opening of the video began with a man sitting on a couch, and he told his story about his single life and how free he felt and happy he was. Then he transitioned to what he called The

Lows, the period of his life where he felt unhappy, which came as no surprise when he mentioned the word marriage. Jacob and I have had our problems in the past, many of which were my own fault because I was having quite a curious eye for other guys. His forgiveness was irrevocable.

The man went on to speak about his wife and kids. How much he felt the spark they had was starting to dim, and how his and her life completely centered around their kids, until they became desperate to find a way to bring the spark back, and have more excitement in their lives without feeling alone while together.

Then came the program.

The part where the pyramid diagram should have been brought up, but it wasn't.

The part where this cult was supposed to choose a variety of items and totems and do enchantments and blessings before the ritual, but they didn't.

Everyone continued to watch the video contently, except for me.

I was the outsider, and the more the man spoke, the more I felt distant to what was going on. The purpose. But the program. The program granted free travel across the country and discounted traveling when going overseas. People would rent houses, such as the ones we are in, and the program pays for it. In return, you recruit, which I suppose is why I was brought here. For recruitment. I'd say that might be as close to cultic as this program gets.

But you'd travel to wherever you wish to go, and you'd

download their application, and search for locals in your area, or even invite friends you may already know. Again, the purpose of my visit was now clear to me. But what did you do?

You'd get to know each other. Meet for the first time, maybe. Go out to eat. Have drinks. Do whatever it was you wanted to with your friends or others in the program, but to complete the purpose of the program was to sleep with each other. But, to sleep with each other wasn't sex. They didn't use that word in the video. They didn't use the word fuck or sexual intercourse. They used "covenant." Their "believers," I guess I could call them that, say that making covenants with multiple people creates a special bond, freeing the wills and temptations from your body that rots within you when you're married. Being able to let go of what you are ashamed of, whether it's multiple partners, cheating habits, sexual pleasures. This program made it *okay*. Or better put, made it seem as though it is okay to actually take part in your temptations.

Successful completion of the program, which included making a covenant and recruiting, equaled payment. Not just a small check of $1,000 after a week or two of work, but add another zero to that. In one evening of making a covenant, as well as recruiting that person or persons, you would have made $12,000 per person recruited. Based off the house we're in, Mike probably owns it, so that only means Mike might have made plenty of covenants to become this wealthy.

The conclusion of the video was, in fact, a porno. Not professional or 4K resolution. More like amateur, recorded-it-yourself homemade videos. Some were three persons, others, four, and another was just two people who were complete strangers until they met earlier that day. I guess that's pretty much what a hookup looked like, but...it was a *covenant.*

Mike pressed a few buttons on the remote once the video ended. The television descended back into the floor, and Mike and Nikki rose from their seats on the couch. They smiled ear to ear, and everyone else clapped. I couldn't. I was still digesting what I saw and heard. I curled one leg over the other, and when I rested my hands between my lap, I hadn't realized the warmth I've managed to muster. Jacob rested his hand on my knee, and when I looked over at him, he was trying to read my face.

"So?" Mike asked as if he had been waiting for me to speak. "What do you think, Simone?" I turned to Mike, and the others waited patiently as well. Tim took a sip from his glass, and Hannah sucked on his pinky finger. Buck curled Kim closer beneath him and she kicked her legs up on the couch. I hadn't noticed she wasn't wearing any shoes, nor did I suspect her to be wearing panties because the glimpse I caught between her legs as her leg went up shoved her clit in my eye.

"I--don't know what to say."

"Say what's on your mind," Jacob told me. "No one's going to judge you for it."

"I almost believe I'm judging all of you just to be

straightforward. Is this why you brought me here?" I wasn't just asking Jacob. I was asking all of them. The strangers in the room who I knew for a fact were nothing like the people I remembered them to be. "You brought me here so one or two of you can fuck m--"

"Make a covenant with you," Nikki interrupted. "A bond. Something that can't be broken, ever. Becoming one with each other."

"Each other?" She nodded.

"Look at it this way," Tim said, and it was the most serious I found him to be the entire night. "Now you can 'cheat' with whoever you want, enjoy free travel, and make money, all at the same time. Who'd pass that up?"

"Who told you I cheated?" I asked him. Tim sipped his drink and eyed Hannah, and she looked at Jacob. Of course, he did. Why else would everyone think I'm the perfect candidate to recruit.

"This your way to not make me feel bad about what I did? You didn't let it go."

"It's not like that," he said. "Covenant aside, just think about those perks."

"This is a scheme. Not a pyramid scheme, but a sexual scheme. I'm in a house with a bunch of swingers."

"At least we accept our lusts rather than run and hide them." I frowned at Nikki then stood.

"And that's your problem, isn't it? You thought I ran and hid from you because I got married, and you were still strutting down a runaway? People probably throw roses at your feet, Nikki. Not all of us are beautifully blessed like you."

"But you are blessed, Simone. I might have all that, but we all share a common thing in here."

"And what's that?" I asked.

"Wanting you, of course. Always been the truth for me." Her eyes leering at me up and down. I couldn't tell if she was just excited to try and recruit me, or if she actually just wanted me. She wasn't the same. "You know I've only dated one man in my life, but my love has always been for you. You can ask Jacob." I turned to him. "He knows."

"Allow me to interrupt for a moment," Mike finally spoke. "Most marriages end in divorce. They all begin with issues that seemed so small in the past, but those things build into worse things as time goes on."

"Worse things like what?"

"Resentment. Wouldn't you love to feel free in your marriage, not worrying about ever losing the one you're with? Knowing that no matter what you do, you will always have Jacob, and he will always have you. Marriages used to be that sacred. That covenant and bond you make when you say your vows, but it's all just words. Some things go wrong, and we know marriage is forever, but many times, it never truly is. If that was the case, why was divorced created? This program seeks to make divorce become obsolete and marriage, truly, forever, as it was designed to be. So let go of all the things that may ruin your marriage and embrace it! Enjoy *others*, but love *Jacob*. That's all it is."

There's truth to what he says. I would know. My parents' divorce ruined everything. My childhood. Where I was to live. Meeting Jacob changed everything. He was the reason, as Nikki puts it, that I ran away. When I cheated, I almost lost Jacob forever. It crushed me. I didn't like that I slept with a stranger, and it hurt him for months. I've always believed he resented me for it because when we were just friends, I was worried that he'd be like most guys. I believed that he would be the one to cheat, and I would be the one who'd have to decide whether to stay or go.

"Will you join us?" Mike asked. For a moment, I found myself actually thinking about it. But I couldn't. Since Jacob knew about this covenant, that could only mean one thing.

"You joined?" I asked him. "You made a covenant before. Is that why you know about all of this, too because I doubt they just told you all of this." Jacob glanced over at the others. He stood up then reached for my wrist.

"I did." I snatched my wrist away.

"With who?" He looked around the room, then stopped on Hannah. "Hannah?" Hannah nodded, and Tim smiled and shrugged.

"He sure did," Tim said. "I made a covenant with Buck and Kim. They made theirs with Mike." I then turned to Nikki.

"And you?" I asked her. "Who did you fuck to join this cult?"

"I made a covenant...Bonded...With nobody."

"Then how do you know so much about all this?"

"Because this is MY program. I have NOT been

strutting down runways, having flowers thrown at my feet, as I let you believe. I was doing this," and she outstretched her arms. "Building an empire from the ground up."

"This is all yours? Your program? Your--business?"

"A successful one at that. When I spoke to Jacob about you, he seemed hurt. I told him I could free him from all of that. That's when I planted the seed. Of course, I didn't make any covenants because I've been saving myself for when he brought you to me. Saving myself for this-- covenant." I nodded and looked over at Jacob, then shook my head.

"I'm leaving."

"Simone?" He whined and grabbed my wrist once more. I took it back again and headed out of the room. He followed closely behind me as I made haste for the door. The second I opened it, he pressed his hand against it and barred me from leaving.

"Let me leave, Jacob."

"You haven't even considered what this program can do for us."

"You mean for you! You already joined! You cheated on me!"

"I made the covenant thinking once you heard about you would join. I figured if I was already in, it would make it easier for you to decide."

"No, you *cheating* made it easier for me to decide."

"Now, that's unfair." He folded his arms across his chest. "You cheated on me first."

"Okay, so we're playing tit-for-tat?"

"No. I'm only saying that I didn't feel great about it, and I only thought you still wanted to be with other people while being with me." I couldn't say anything. I was feeling a mix between anger and sympathy for him.

"I only love you, Jacob."

"I know, but I also know you have a wandering eye. Now, I forgave you for what you have done, and I only wish to always be with you no matter what. It's just-- if we don't at least make our relationship as open as everyone in the program's, then I don't know how we would last. It's not like you told me you cheated. I had to find out for myself, just as you did, and this program breaks the need of keeping things secret. We can do as we wish, and know at the end of the day where our heart rest rather than questioning it all the time."

I forced myself to nod. He had a point. Would it have hurt so much if I expected it all along, yet know he only loves me? I might have been overthinking it, but he put the truth in my face, making it undeniable. I did have a wandering eye, but I loved Jacob. I've always forced him to do things he didn't want to do, but at least this meant he meant he was trying to keep us together, saying it was alright for me to have this wandering eye, but to allow him the same respect I give, to be free from the temptations without reaping any consequences.

"Okay," I finally said.

"Okay?"

I nodded. "I'll do it. I'll make a covenant."

Chapter 4: The Covenant

Jacob led me back to the room, and everyone was still where they sat when I left. Mike smiled when he saw that I returned, and Nikki smirked and sipped from a drink she must've just made.

"The prodigal Simone has returned," Tim said as he raised his glass."

"I'll do it," I told Mike. Mike nodded and smiled. He then turned to his butler, and his butler nodded.

"I'll make the preparations for the room," he told Mike. I wasn't sure what to expect, but everyone seemed to spring to life and started moving. Buck threw

Kim over his shoulders, and as she kicked and laughed, he slapped her ass. Tim curled Hannah under his arm, but he couldn't keep one hand off his drink.

"I'm going to need this," he said, taking breathless, heaping gulps. "It'll numb me a bit to make me last longer." Mike removed his suit coat from his back as he led us back to the stairs as Nikki trailed behind Jacob and I, carrying a bottle and a few cups. She started preparing a drink on the way there.

"Where are we going?"

"To make the covenant."

"So, that's what I saw earlier."

Nikki nodded. "Yes. That's why I didn't want you to disrupt them. A covenant isn't all about sex. It's about acceptance, forming an unbreakable bond."

"I just--"

"I know," Nikki said. "It's hard to believe in something when you're used to something else. It will take some practice, but soon, you won't look at us like we're strangers, and you'll actually feel like one of us too. Happier." Jacob smiled and nodded, then Nikki handed me one of the cups. "Drink this."

It didn't look like an average drink because of the color. A lime green. I thought she must've put something in it.

"What's that?" I asked.

"It'll help you get into it. You don't look like you're ready for what's about to happen." I grimaced, but she was right. I wasn't being led to some random party in another room. I was being led to a covenant, making a unique bond with seven others. Without a second longer of hesitation, I accepted the drink.

"Be sure to chug it," Jacob added. I nodded and started tossing it back. It was more like a smoothie texture than some juice. A tint of mint, but smelled of spinach and arugula. A tad bit sour with an aftertaste of a pinch of something spicy. It didn't taste great at all, but in the amount of time it took me to take the last drop from the bottom of the cup, the stairs extended into heaven, high into the ceiling, like something out of a dream. Before I could stammer up the steps, Jacob caught me by one arm, and Nikki caught me by the other.

"You'll be fine," Jacob said, his face in doubles and triples.

"You will be," Nikki said, and her face did the same. They smiled, and their voices echoed like as if we were in a tunnel. I might have been seeing things doubling, tripling, and even quadrupling, but I felt more alive than I had ever felt. The marble floor beneath my feet felt like I was walking on clouds. When they led me into the room, a bright light met my eyes, and I might have thought, only for a moment, I was heaven.

I heard moans, but I still couldn't see. I felt Jacob and Nikki's hands all over me, taking off my shirt, pulling down my jeans, and removing my bra. The moans got louder and louder as they led me by the hands again until I was able to see. They lay me down on the bed, and the cushions were soft between my fingers as I pulled myself up towards the headboard. They were already naked, and I wasn't sure if they had gotten undressed while we walked up the stairs, or if they did as they got me down to my panties.

They stood at the end of the bed in front of me, giving me a show. Tim, Mike, and Jacob jerked their dicks, standing on each side of me, while Hannah, Kim, and Nikki gave me a seductive dance and sway of their hips. They played with each others' breasts, licking the nipple and giggling. As the boys jerked themselves, they groaned and bit down on their lips, their eyes only on me. I was the special guest of the night and had assumed they must be only catering to me.

There was only three men there. I knew that for sure, but the drink multiplied them, and I felt I was among a large group of them. Nikki climbed atop of my face and sat on it. She grinded against my lips, and I felt more hands than I could count all over my body. My breasts were squeezed. Nipples played with then sucked by a warm, wet mouth. The mouth pulled and even bit down on my nipple. I was squirming on the bed like a worm. But others held me down by the legs, caressing up my inner thighs until someone shoved their tongue down my throat.

I couldn't keep up with the overwhelming lust that everyone secreted naturally. Too much pleasure in massive bursts all at once on different areas of my body. I had to stop nibbling on Nikki's clit when someone started chewing on mine. I couldn't help but moan. The boys came around closer, leaning forward for me to pleasure them. So I did. The way I've always pleased Jacob whenever I could as he drove.

I let them into my mouth, gripping both hands around two of them, and my mouth on the third. When I heard a moan, I knew I must've been pleasing Jacob. I could recognize that throaty moan among any. I gripped my lips tighter around him, swirling my tongue in circles around his girth, jerking Tim and Mike. Then, large hands turned me over. It must've been Buck. The hands gripped entirely around my ankles as he pulled me to the center of the bed. The covers and sheets folded beneath everyone, and I wasn't the only one moaning anymore. Tim shoved his drunken self inside of Kim, as Buck ate me like a meal. Jacob kissed and sucked on Hannah's breasts, and Nikki and Mike sixty-nined beside me. We moaned together, and I couldn't help but feel myself sinking into the bed itself.

That drink. That drink did the most to me. As smooth as it was, it only made me wetter than I was used to feeling. I felt myself leaking as a faucet, but Buck didn't back down one bit. His tongue explored every inch inside of me, and he nibbled on my clit as if he never knew the existence of food. I couldn't contain it anymore. As early in the covenant as it was, I was already cumming in Buck's mouth as he hungrily ate me, and his beard prickled the inner thighs and gave them a slight tickle that made me lock at the knee. I kicked my legs up, but then Buck switched with Hannah.

As she ate me, she kept her ass up, putting a deep arch in her back. I didn't know she could get that flexible. She moved her hair back, and Buck crawled up behind her. Mike crawled over my face, and though I didn't see Buck thrust inside of Hannah, I knew he must've because the moan that escaped Hannah's throat stopped her from licking the cum out of me. Mike shoved his dick into my throat, not giving me a chance to take a breather from pleasing Jacob. As Kim bent herself over Hannah, staying vulnerable for Buck to do as he pleased, she used my hips to keep herself steadily arched.

Hannah was the first to drop. She came on Buck, and he had Kim lick what was left of her. As she passed out, I was put in her place, and Tim traded places with Buck, bending me over in front of him. It was my turn to be filled, and it was my turn to please Kim. She lied herself down, her tits jiggled side to side as she moved. Jacob held her arms back, caressing his hands slowly across her arms as Mike held and squeezed her breasts in his hand. Tim helped me thrust myself against Buck as Buck couldn't contain himself any longer. His groans almost sounded monstrous. Throaty. Deep. Growling.

He collapsed beside Hannah, and Tim took no more than a second to fill himself inside of me. He might not have been as big as Buck, but he sure knew about the motion of the ocean. He grinded against me, pulling some of himself out, teasing my clit with the tip, before shoving himself back inside of me. He held his girth there, allowing me to feel and grip every inch, and when he pulled himself out, he jerked until his cum covered both of my ass cheeks.

I was getting sore, but I loved it. I helped Kim climb atop of Jacob, and as she rode him, I played and licked her breasts. She scratched along his gorilla-sized chest as he held her by the hips. Mike must've enjoyed the show because he sat back in one of the chairs and only pleased himself, watching with a male gaze glean in his eye. His lips quivered as he jerked, and his shaft stood tall like the Eiffel until he exploded in his hands and slumped to rest.

As Kim rode Jacob, I kissed and sucked into her neck, spooning her motions. She held my head to her shoulder as she tossed her head back. Jacob reached and pulled us both forward, and we played tonsil hockey with each other. Kim's giggles squeezed in between our lips, but then her giggles turned to moans again, and her eyebrows converged as her mouth dropped. The look she gave Jacob told us she was giving in. He was making her tap out. She quivered as she rode him, grinding then shaking in place before she toppled to the side.

Jacob was still stiff as a pool stick.

I took Kim's place happily, having a second round with the one I truly love. His eyes told me he knew I'd enjoy this, and he was right. I had to admit that much. He thrusted against my grind, our juices mixed between us. Before I could get into it, he put me on my back and climbed on top. He thrusted himself against me as I kept my legs high, his sweat made his body clam up, and the heat he gave off did the same to mine. Unlike the others, I wasn't just fucking Jacob. I was making love to him.

The next morning, I woke up next to him and only him. The others must've gotten up early and quiet. Music boomed through the hallway, and the smell of bacon and eggs lingered. I turned over and curled one leg around Jacob, and he opened his eyes and smiled.

"Sleep well?" he asked. I kissed him and smiled.

"You know I did."

"Good." He staggered himself to a sit and stretched and yawned. "Let's get breakfast."

~

The rest of the weekend was more than anything I could have expected. I felt myself growing closer to everyone. Mike held a barbeque when the sun finally decided to come out. We took his boat out on the lake, and Tim taught me how to fish. He said his Pop was a fisherman, and even though he didn't follow in his footsteps, fishing was in his family's blood. Hannah taught me how to bujo. Bullet journaling will really come in handy when I try to organize my life and goals. Buck showed all of his old college football highlights. I have to say, the man could have been in the NFL if he didn't get injured, but he's happily married to Kim with a couple of kids, coaching high school football. Kim told me about her new marketing business for entrepreneurs, helping them increase their earning potential. Even though these people have this program to fall back on, they never put a pause on their lives. They only enhanced it. Jacob gathered our bags and program start-up packet by the door, and Mike followed behind with the others. We were the first to leave, and I didn't want to.

"Hey," Mike said, as we walked out. "Don't slouch your face, Simone. I have a feeling we'll be doing this again sometime."

I smiled back and nodded. "The feeling is mutual."

Between the Cheeks

Chapter 1: Sugar and Spice

She held up her legs as I pounded her harder. Deeper! *FASTER!* She was in for it and had no idea. Do I still have it? She asked if I still had it. *Of course I still had it! I'm still young!* I can be spontaneous in bed as I was when we were teens. I can still spice things up and please her as I've always had.

She moaned and tossed her head back and forth. *Moaning and moaning! Ohhhh, she was loving it! Did I still have it? Ha!* Should see the look on your face right now. I've certainly proved you wrong, Bryce. *I. Still. Have. It.*

I came. Nut busted right inside of her, filling her up like a crispy cream. I collapsed over her, trying to catch my breath, trying to slow my heartbeat, but all I could do was laugh. Laugh at the fact that Bryce asked if I still have it.

Do I still have it?

I rolled off of her and onto the bedsheets, still heaving my breaths as she turned away and curled the covers over her shoulder. Something was off. I clearly showed I still had it. I just performed like a talented elephant in a circus, impossibly balancing myself on a small ball that surely should have popped. I performed like a magician, fooling an entire audience, forcing them to believe I could not possibly be human yet something else. I took her to the moon and back with that performance and all she did was turn away and cover herself?!

Something was wrong.

"Bryce?" I said. She gave me the side of her face, peering over at me in the corner of her blue eyes through her short black hair bangs.

"Hmm?"

Hmm. HMM? What did she mean by...HMM? Not yes, master? Or yes, daddy? Or even something as corny and mushy as yes, honey or pumpkin? But HMM? She waited for me to respond, but I was still stuck on her's. As she glared at me through her hair, putting her chin against her shoulder, not even trying to turn towards me and give her the rest of her face, she sighed. *She sighed.* And that's all she needed to do. That told me everything. That sigh told me what was wrong.

"You were faking it," I said as I sat up in bed. "Weren't you?" She didn't respond immediately. I thought that maybe, just maybe, for once, she would lie to me and make me feel good about it, but Bryce wasn't one to lie. If she didn't like something, she told me. If she did like something, she'd speak about it for weeks, and after the look, she gave and turned away from me again, was her way of telling me she faked it. "I can help you finish. Grab your vibrator, and I'll help you finish."

She shook her head. "It's alright, Jonathan. Don't worry about it, really." I couldn't believe it. I surely put my heart and soul into that and still didn't get anywhere with it. She used to allow me to help her finish, but even that changed. I couldn't let her down again. I needed to find a solution.

"How about we spice things up more?" I asked. She gave me the side of her face again and sighed.

"How, Jonathan?"

"I don't know." I shrugged. "More positions?" She didn't answer, so I took it as a go. High school missionary position surely wasn't going to get me any points in bed with my own girlfriend. That position only worked early on, but back then, I remembered it to be much more fun.

The next night, I was ready. I had prepared myself as if it were a first date. I showered with music to get myself hyped, gelled my hair back to achieve that bad boy greaser look, practiced my male gaze, peering through my eyebrows with a smirk. I had the look, the smell, and only needed to perform. When she got off work, I had everything prepared at home for a great evening.

I wore the suit I took her to the prom in, hoping that when she saw me dressed in the tailored, blue suit and tie, she'll relive the memory of that night, the night we first gave ourselves to each other. I had her favorite Riesling, Dr. Frank's semi-dry, standing beside the vase of roses I gotten earlier in the day. Her favorite dish, steak, covered in sauteed mushrooms, and garlic parmesan mashed potatoes rested at both heads of the red covered dining table.

The car pulled into the driveway, and when I peered out the window, she looked exhausted. Things couldn't get any better or more in my favor. She had no idea of the night she was going to have. She'd be happy again, remembering how much of a great man she decided to marry. There would be no further need for me to prove myself. She opened the door, carrying her purse on her arm, and began taking off her boots.

"I'm home," she said, and her voice barely carried past the doorway. *Look up*, I kept thinking to myself. *Look up and see me standing here in the suit.* She was so fixated on taking off her boots, she hadn't taken a glance at me yet. She slung her purse to the side, and when the couch caught it, she finally acknowledged my presence. Her jaw hung as her eyes gazed at me up in down. I knew she'd love it. I knew she'd love seeing me in this suit. I peered down at myself, smiled at my own cunningness, and her stunned jaw morphed into a smile that stretched across her face.

"You look like a grease-ball getting ready to meet the Don," she giggled. Well, it was better than her saying she didn't like that I wore a suit, but it still hurt to see she might not even recognized the suit anymore.

"Do you...like it?" I asked, turning in circles, hoping that she would realize *what* suit it was. She shrugged and smiled.

"I guess. Where did you get it? It looks a little small." Granted I might have gained a few pounds since high school, I suppose the fitting did wrap tight around the stomach and arms. From my Dad. She knew that. It was the suit he married Mom in, and I was blessed to have this suit for prom.

"It doesn't matter," I told her, forcing myself to smile. "Come eat." As bad as I wanted to tell her about the suit, I had to get things moving. The suit was only a small piece to the full, sweet pie I was going to give her later on.

When we entered the room, she raised her eyebrows in surprise, only the surprise didn't seem to be a positive one. She smelled the roses, and her nose stiffened. She peered down at the meal and grimaced.

"Jonathan, you do know I've changed diets."

"Yes," I said, "but you can still have some of it."

"There's too much fat around the steak, and the mashed potatoes are swimming in its grease. How much of our money did you spend on this steak anyways, Jonathan?" It always seemed that I could never do anything right in her eyes lately. Too many dishes in the sink. Why are your clothes on the floor?

When do you plan on getting off the game so we can watch a show? Slowly, but surely, the perfect evening I had planned was beginning to look unpromising.

"No worries," I told her and clasped my hands together. "We can skip dinner and maybe I get something else from the store."

"And spend more of the money we need to save?" She shook her head. "No, it's alright. I'll just peck at the mushrooms." And she did. She ate her plate like bird, pecking at small pieces, yet it barely looked like she had eaten anything at all. She pushed her plate away, and I smiled, hoping to ease the mood. I took her plate and put the leftovers in a container. When I came back into the dining room from placing it in the fridge, she was turning the music off and undoing her dress.

"Going to shower," she said. I thought I might have made her upset and hoped she'd ask for me to join her. She didn't.

I waited on the bed for her, watching the crack in the bathroom door as she showered. I had gotten myself out of the suit and found myself daydreaming of better days, dreaming of the past when we both were far too excited to shower together, eat whatever our hearts desired, and fucked like bunnies. When the shower turned off, it brought me back to the bedroom in my pajamas. It was quiet for a moment, but then the bathroom door opened, and the light sprang onto me. For once, she smiled at me, and I smiled back. Maybe all she wanted all along was a chance to get out of her work clothes and shower. I might have bombarded her with my neediness, and it only increased her frustrations.

"I'm sorry I was a bad sport, Jonathan. I was just exhausted." So I was right, and I'm sure as hell glad I was. It wasn't really about the fact I was wearing a suit she didn't recognize or the fact that I spent money on a steak dinner, neglecting her diet. She was tired.

"It's fine."

"I'll make it up to you," she said. She uncoiled the towel around her and showed me her naked, slender body, her breasts, firm and pink, her nipples hardened as I looked at them. She gave a slight sway of her hips, grinding against the towel. A deep crease between her thighs led the path to the stubble, shaved hair over her clit, and she dipped her hips, coming down to a squat, opening her legs to show me her pussy lips. I leaned back on the bed, lusting for her to climb atop of me. She must've read my mind. She gazed into my eyes and prowled over me like a lioness. She pursed her lips as the soapy, mint and evergreen aroma scent lingered from her damp body.

Her lips kissed into my neck as she held my head back, gripping handfuls of my hair, grinding against my erected cock through my pajamas. She shoved me back and ran her fingers down my chest hungrily. My heart was throbbing. I wanted her more than I could ever remember. More than anything. I just wanted to fuck her already, to show her I still have it.

She leaned over me, putting her breast in my mouth, and as I sucked, she dug her hand into my pajamas and gripped my cock. She caressed and jerked it, making my cock wet, then sucked the pre-cum off her fingers. She pulled it through the crotch hole and slid me inside of her. We gasped together as she slowly slid down every inch until I couldn't go any deeper. She tossed her head back, and her breasts and chest turned crimson. I gripped handfuls of her breasts, gave her my first thrust...and then it happened. It should not have happened, but it did. I wanted to cry inside. Everything was just seeming to fall into place and I just couldn't contain myself longer than a minute.

I came.

It only took her a few moments to realize it happened. She exhaled, and all the excitement I had given her drained from her face. I couldn't even last long enough to put her into another position. I got far too excited and wanted her so much that the buildup was too great. I felt my soul leave my body.

"Bryce, I--"

"It's alright, Jonathan," she said with a drag. She climbed off of me, and the cum spilled out of her and dripped onto my thigh and the bedsheets. She went back into the bathroom without another word. I tossed my head back and shook my head. Maybe I don't have it after all.

Chapter 2: Exit Only

With Christmas just days away, I had to find some other way to please Bryce. What better than a bunch of gifts. I know she doesn't want me to spend any more money, especially after buying that expensive steak dinner we barely enjoyed, but I became desperate. I needed a Christmas miracle, so I decided I would have to create my own.

I spent much of that day at the mall. I did more window shopping than actually shopping. The giant Christmas tree in the center of the mall stood as high as the ceiling, and children ran circles around it, dressed in their tight coats and choking scarves as they laughed and played while parents sat and gossiped.

I went from jewelry stores to clothing stores, back to jewelry stores, only to go into a phone store, before I realized I had no idea how to shop. I had grown used to going out with Bryce and she'd have all these ideas on where we would go, what we needed to buy, all while staying within a budget that kept us comfortable. I needed help, and I sure wasn't going to ask. I could handle it, I thought, but lucky for me, my Christmas miracle arrived when my phone buzzed as I was peering through the glass of Victoria's Secret. I recognized the number, but couldn't figure out who it belonged to.

"Hello?" I answered.

"You look like one of those creepy guys who stare into lingerie stores as if you'd see some boobs pop out." I peered at my phone, confused, but I did recognize the voice. "It's been a while, Jonathan."

"Melinda?" I asked, finally grasping onto the voice. "How'd you know I was--"

"Turn around, silly," she giggled. I turned and saw her standing outside of a clothing store, waving her hand above her head. She had bags that almost ran up both of her arms. Her big, red hair ran down her red coat that had large black buttons down the front. I hadn't seen her since I could remember. I hung up the phone and zig-zagged through the crowd with a smile on my face. I barely made it through the crowd, and Melinda had already dropped her bags and threw her arms around me.

"I haven't seen you in years!" I exclaimed. "What are you doing here in Maine? I thought you moved to Arizona to get away from the weather."

"I did," she said and smiled. "Back for the holidays. Doing some shopping. I see yours is going pretty well." She peered at my hands. Still empty.

"Right. Well, since my hands are obviously free, let me carry some of those for you."

"You don't have to."

"Yes, I do." I took a few of the bags in each hand, and she smiled. "What store were you heading to next?"

"I just finished, actually. I was going to get a holiday peppermint mocha from Starbucks."

"I could use one of those."

"Join me so we can catch up. Maybe you can tell me all about your adventures at Victoria's Secret," she joked.

When we got our drinks, we sat at one of the tables in the crowded food court. We didn't say much at first, only peering up from our drinks to smile and look around awkwardly. I guess this was catching up. She looked like she hadn't aged a day. Vampire genes. Crimson hair. Minty, green eyes. Red lipstick that matched her fingernails.

"So," I finally said, breaking the silence. "How's life in Arizona? Everything you expected?"

"As in no snow. It's perfect. There's a mountain everywhere you go. The heat isn't as humid as it gets here in the summer. I think only miss Maine in the winter."

"Which, if I remember correctly, is why you left, to get away from this cold."

"Oh, yes. That's for sure."

"How's the tech business going? They promote you to CEO yet?" She laughed and shook her head.

"Not yet, but we are onto something big." And her face lit up. She placed her cup down on the table, and sat back, crossing one leg over the other, and damn her legs were long. "We're developing a new kind of service for cell phones, homes, and entertainment."

"Like what exactly?"

"Well, I can't go into detail too much, or you just may steal the idea yourself." She winked. "But I will say it will revolutionize the way people use their cell phones and streaming entertainment. Wifi will be a thing of the past, and this technology will push a new foundation of cell phone operating and turn the internet into something tangible rather than digital."

"Wow," was all I could muster. Melinda was never the stereotype "dumb blonde." She was always quite the opposite. An inventor. An innovator. Someone who cared about the future world more than she did about the past and present moment. She laughed and smiled, and then she rested her hand on mine. I clocked the golden wedding ring on her finger.

"Married too?" I asked, moving to a completely different topic.

"You almost sounded sad saying it," she said. "Could ask you the same." She clocked my finger, and it was naked. "But I might already know."

"Well, not quite there," I told her. "Working on it, though." She withdrew her hand and her smile gleamed.

"That's good for you. See, I knew you would meet somebody."

"Well, hopefully, your love life is going better than mine."

"We have our problems."

"In mine, I am the problem." She frowned a bit and leaned her head to the side.

"I'm sure there's more to it than that."

"Oh, no," I assured her. "It's all me."

"What are you doing exactly?" I couldn't respond immediately. Was far too embarrassed to say. Besides, what business did I have telling Melinda about my performance in bed?

That topic is a sacred place between partners. Moreover, what could she possibly say or do to help me change the way things were? The problem lied in my penis. It needed to perform better. "Jonathan?"

"Sorry," I told her. "It's stupid."

"It can't be that stupid if it bothers you," she assured. "It's gotta be something serious, especially if we're talking about you eventually proposing to this girl." I still couldn't respond. I only stared back into her eyes, and she mustered a soft smile. "Tell me. I could probably help."

But she had a point. Getting her perspective might be a good chance to hear something from a female's perspective that I wasn't hearing from Bryce herself. Melinda was always there for me when I needed something. From homework answers to test cheating, even some pointers on dancing at prom, she practically helped me with some fresh moves that swoon Bryce enough to go home with me.

"Alright," I said and sipped from my cup. She held her cup in both hands and gave a slight dance in the chair. "Don't laugh."

"I promise."

"Okay. I'm just going to come out and say it." She nodded. "I'm going to put it as simple as possible." She nodded again, only this time her eyes squinted a bit. "Just going to spit it out."

"Wait," she said, and she lowered her voice. She leaned over the table and stared me square in the eye. "Are you having problems because...you're gay?"

"Gay? What? No!"

"Oh," and she leaned back in her chair then giggled. "Okay, I thought you were about to come out to me, but just tell me already. What's the problem?" I sighed and dropped my shoulders.

"I can't please Bryce in bed," I mumbled. She quirked her head to the side.

"What?"

"I said, I can't please Bryce in bed." She froze. Here it comes, I thought to myself. The part where she laughs. The part where I embarrass myself and walk away.

"That's…" Only she didn't laugh. She didn't do as much as chuckle. "Quite a problem."

"Tell me about it."

"Can you...get it up?" She asked, and I almost felt like I was talking about a private matter to my doctor.

"I can get it up. It's not that. It's just--last night I came in seconds. It doesn't usually happen, I just got really excited, but anyway, besides the major point. She's just-- unsatisfied." Melinda nodded then sipped from her cup.

"I see. It sounds like you just need some new moves. More foreplay. More buildup into it."

"The only time she cums is when she touches herself." She almost spat out her coffee. That was the laughter I was looking for.

"That *is* a problem. You need to spice things up asap, Jon or the worst is yet to come."

"The worst? What do you mean by that?"

She sighed. "Well, if you can't please her in bed, you may lose her entirely. Sex is an important part of partnership, and if she feels you can't do so much as perform, even just the slightest, well, I don't know the kind of girl she is, but you may lose her."

"But I don't want to lose her. I thought maybe more positions would do."

"Depends on those positions, but I think you need more than that in your arsenal. If you want to spice things up, then SPICE things up. Don't add more positions and call it spicing things up. More positions is just--more positions."

"Well, how exactly do I-- spice things up."

"By being extra spontaneous."

"Extra spontaneous."

"Mhmm."

"What would be extra spontaneous?"

"Plenty of things, but one in particular to start...I'll say just come out and say it. Plain and simple."

I nodded. "Yeah?"

"You bend her over and fuck her in the ass." This time, I was the one who froze. I couldn't believe what I just heard, but she definitely said it. She finished her drink then placed the empty cup in the center of the table. "You know?" she asked as if she thought I didn't know what she was saying.

"Yeah, I know I just can't fathom that you said I should do that."

"Do what? Fuck her in the ass?"

"Yes. That exactly. Fuck her in the ass."

"Mhmm." She nodded again.

"I always thought that was a do not enter, exit-only space?"

"Who made that rule? Listen, if you want to spice things

up, you have to be willing to try all possible solutions, and I just gave you one."

"What if she isn't into that kind of thing. I mean, I don't even know if I am."

"It may just be what keeps her from leaving in the end game. It was only a suggestion, but it's up to you to decide what you're going to do." Melinda might have been right. Just from my performance in bed, Bryce was already showing signs of our disconnection, and it was only getting worse. She had grown quiet around me, easily frustrated with me, unwilling to do much of anything if it had anything to do with me. It was just me, the problem. I guess she did seem down for the spicing-things-up part, so I guess that means she might even be open to it. Either way, it was worth considering.

"How do I go about practicing this? With some sex doll?" Melinda then had this glean in her eye. It was until she had responded when I realize how she could possibly know what I could do to spice things up.

"I'll help you."

I shook my head, confused. "I'm sorry. What do you mean by HELP me?"

"Practice. You need to practice."

"And...you're basically saying you'll be my dummy doll?" She nodded. "Melinda, that crosses so many boundaries I can't even get into."

"You need to practice. Anal isn't just as easy as sliding your penis into her rectum. If you don't know what you're doing, all you'll do is drive her away...in pain...in her ass. Are you not attracted to me? Is that it?"

"No, no, no. Quite the opposite, actually. I shouldn't even be saying that much, but I mean, you're married. I plan to get engaged."

"Look," and she rested her hand atop of mine again. "I've always been there for you when you needed help, and I'm doing that now. We don't have to tell anyone anything. It would be between us, and afterward, we could forget it ever happened."

"Forget I shoved myself into your ass...Sounds easy."

She giggled. "I'm just being a friend, trying to save my friend from losing the love of his life. Wouldn't you do anything to keep her?"

"Of course, I would."

"Then you may have to realize this may be one of those things. Besides, I owe you anyway. You helped me heal from a toxic relationship, and now I've met and married someone I love with my soul. Helping you wouldn't change that." It took me a while before I was able to give her a straightforward answer. I couldn't keep Bryce's disappointment out of my head, the look she had every night I tried to please her. I ran out of my own ideas, and when the opportunity for a new one arrives, I run away? I couldn't. A beautiful friend of mine was going to help me save my pending engagement. No strings attached. Secret.

"Alright," I finally said. "Help me."

Chapter 3: Practice Makes Perfect

Melinda was an expert at foreplay. Without any strings attached, it was almost as if she were in love my cock. She gripped it with both hands, caressing it up and down, swirling her hands in opposite directions. She sucked the tip with her lips and smacked on me like a treat.

"You've---done this---a lot--haven't you?" I gasped.

"Mhmm," she moaned as she sucked, then her mouth popped when she released me. "If we're going to do this, I have to get you as erect as possible. That's how you'll be when you're with her. Can't go into this with a limp dick." She started sucking again, and I gasped.

"Well...I almost believe you're also enjoying this too much." She didn't respond. She jerked me again, then tied her hair back with her hair tie. When it was away from her face, she traced the tip of her tongue from my sack up to the tip. It made my toes curl, and my body tense up. It almost tickled.

"Alright," she said. "Got you nice and hard." She jerked me off a few more times, then played with the pre-cum between her fingernails. She tasted them. *Yeah. Definitely enjoying this more than I thought she would.* She then removed her clothes, tossing them off the bed, showing me busty, perfect, perky breasts. Her body was as slender as Bryce's, but her hips had a much deeper curve in them. I almost felt myself more attracted to her than Bryce, but I had to keep my head on the purpose of all this. It wasn't to enjoy Melinda. It was to learn.

She then threw her face into her pillow then arched her back. She had a deep arch. It almost looked as if she could bend and snap herself in half at will. Both of her cheeks jiggled as she gave them a twerk and giggled. She then smacked both of her cheeks, then gripped them in her hands and spread them. Her pussy opened and showed her pink, deep hole. Her ass spread, but the crack was tight and possibly fit a needle. It only made me harder as she then put lube on the tips of her fingers and massaged it right on the crack.

"Lube it just enough to help you slip in." As she did, I couldn't help but look at how wet she was making herself. She might have actually been trying to tease me. I wanted to shove myself inside of her pussy, but the boundary was already determined. No vaginal penetration. This was all practice. She then peered over her shoulder and seen I was frozen in place. She smiled and sighed. "One thrust," she said. "Just once because I know you want to. By the way you're looking at it, just don't bust right after." She put her face back down onto the bed. "I'll help you."

She reached beneath herself and grabbed a hold of my cock. She jerked it a bit, then rubbed my tip against her clit. She then used her other hand to open her pussy lips more as she slowly put me inside of her. I slid right in there as if my cock was on ice. She moaned, and I shoved all of girth and length. Then she pulled herself up the bed, away from me, and I slipped right out.

"Alright," she said, catching her breath. "Focus. Back to work." I almost wanted to cum already. She spread her cheeks again, and I put a bit more of lube on the crack of her ass. I massaged it, and it seemed easy enough doing so. The lube started to milk and cream itself. "Slowly, put the tip in. Slowly."

I tried pushing the tip right against her tight crack, and when I felt I could slip right in, I pushed in deeper, but she sprang forward and gasped.

"Too fast, Jonathan. Just because it seems you can just slide right in doesn't mean you should."

"Sorry," I said. She then turned over and sat before me.

"Have to keep you hard." She jerked and sucked me more until I was fully erect again from failure. She lied on her back, then threw her long legs behind her head. I didn't know she was flexible. She played with herself, then dabbed the lube I placed already. She held her ass cheeks with her own hands and spread them. Her pussy lips quivered open a bit as well. "Try again."

I nodded. I placed my tip against her crack again. She spread her cheeks as wide as she could, and this time, my tip slipped in. When she gasped, I stopped. She smiled and nodded for me to go deeper. I kept going slowly, and I gasped with her. It was much tighter than her pussy. It practically ate me and pulled me in more. She gripped and quivered around it, watching as I kept going. She put her head back and closed her eyes tight. "Now ease back, then try and get it all in." I nodded and pulled back. "Slow. Remember, you can't go full throttle until you build the depth."

I slide back slow, and when I could see half of my tip, I slid back in until I was able to get all of me inside of her. When I saw and felt it was alright to stroke back and forth slowly, I felt myself getting ready to cum.

"Now...you...can...go...faster." She held her cheeks open still as I started putting more force into my stroke. My chest heated like a furnace as I tried to keep from cumming. Her face got redder by the second, and I thought I might have been hurting her. I stopped for a moment, but then she tried to pull me back in.

"No," she moaned. "Don't stop." She was enjoying it. She looked like she was about to cry. I listened and kept stroking, reading her face as she looked as if she was about to cry. "Fuck....Jon," she moaned. I kept going, then sped up. She let go of her cheeks and started rubbing across her clit vigorously. That's when her slight moans turned into full-fledged whimpers and screams. "Faster...Faster!" I thrusted into her, and her eyes looked as if they were going to roll in the back of her head. She tossed her head back, then tossed her head forward and kept rubbing. Tossed it back. Tossed it forward. Cried. I tossed my head back, not able to contain it anymore, then I felt the grip around my cock sink into a wet pool. She gripped and convulsed around my cock, cumming with me as I released. She threw her head back, wiped the sweat from her face, and shivered as I slowly pulled myself out of her. When my tip came out, her crack gaped open and cum spilled out of it and onto the end of the bedsheet.

"How was that?" I asked, trying to catch my breath. She nodded.

"Oh, yes. You're ready. Trust me. If she doesn't love you after that, you need another woman. Maybe I'll be a free agent again."

Chapter 4: All or Nothing

The time to redeem myself came. I planned out the evening the same way it was planned days ago. Flowers were bought, but they weren't roses. I don't believe she liked the roses before, so this time, I got chrysanthemums. They're a symbol for hope, so they were my good luck charm. No steak dinner with mushrooms and mashed potatoes. Instead, chopped, arugula salad with carrots, cucumber, and strips of grilled, unseasoned chicken to rid away the salt. The wine was the only thing that remained the same. She had to have her Dr. Frank's semi-dry Riesling. No blue suit and tie.

Instead, I kept it plain and simple...Pajamas.

Melinda told me it may be best to remind Bryce of the man she fell in love with as well as show her the man I am today. Completely relying on a past time to show my love was just as bad as holding onto a past that no longer existed. This similar, but different approach had to be what saved us. If this didn't work, then perhaps our relationship wouldn't either. She might not have been satisfied with me for a while, but her sex drive has always been the same. I had to take that into consideration for sure. Sexual satisfaction is important in relationships, but sexual satisfaction is important to Bryce in general.

When she pulled into the driveway, I almost had deja vu. I remembered how disconnected she was early on because I shoved dinner and my neediness in her face. This time, I was going to take another approach on presentation. When the door opened, I was there to greet her.

"Jonathan? You scared me for a moment."

I smiled and kissed her. "Sorry, my love." I took her purse and held the door open for her to step inside. Once she did, I rested her purse on the couch, then bent over and removed her boots. She rested her hand on my back, and I placed them to the side.

"I'll run your shower." She smiled, and the frustrations I'm used to seeing when she walked in the door was absent. Without another word, I headed upstairs and started her shower water. I heard her footsteps come up the stairs, and when she came into the bathroom, she wrapped her arms around me and rested her head against my back.

After her shower, she came back down the stairs in her gown. As she joined me at the table, she smelled the flowers and smiled. She gazed down at the food, and her eyes widened with approval. She then sat and had her wine.

We spent the evening watching rom-coms. I wanted to get her into the mood as much as possible. Melinda taught me that foreplay doesn't just begin with kissing. Foreplay begins with setting the mood, something people tend to neglect doing. It really gives a great head start well before getting to the bedroom. When she started curling her arms around my neck, I knew the movies were making her feel warm and fuzzy inside. I carried her up the stairs and to the bedroom.

I laid her down onto her back and pushed her legs apart. She smiled up at me as I pulled my shirt from over my head and tossed it aside. I showed her how hard I was, pressing my pajamas against my crotch. She rubbed up her body, and when she got to her shoulder straps, she pulled her gown from over her head and lay there naked before me.

I got down on my knees and placed my head between her legs, licking her inner thighs, tracing circles with my tongue before nibbling and sucking at her skin. She gasped and squirmed against my beard stubble, and as I breathed, her legs shook. I pushed them wider, and her pussy lips parted. I feasted on her, nibbled on her clit, gripping her breasts in my hands as she grinded against my face. I pulled and tugged on her clit with my lips, and it snatched itself back between her pussy lips before I pulled on it again. Each flick from my tongue made her shake. She gripped handfuls of my hair and forced me to devour her. I grabbed her by the wrists and pinned her hands down, and kept licking and tasting her. She couldn't escape. Just before I thought she might cum for the first time in a while, I stood up and pulled down my pajamas.

My cock rocked back and forth and bounced up and down with heaviness. The veins sharpened around it. She sprang up to a seat and started sucking, jerking me at the same time. Her warm, wet mouth caressed around it, and she playfully tried to wrap her tongue around it. She giggled, and I smiled down at her, holding the back of her head with my hand, guiding her pace. I tried to reach deep into her throat, and as I did, she looked up at me with her beautiful eyes and tried to take it. Her eyes got teary, and I pushed myself further and deeper into her throat. I held it there for a moment, throbbing like a heartbeat. Before she could choke, I pulled myself out, and she caught her breath before sucking again. She tried pulling my soul out of me, sucking hard enough to pull me forward.

I pushed her back on the bed, and she threw her legs open. I felt myself wanting to cum already, but I had to hold it. When I shoved myself inside of her, I fell in deep. Her head tossed back, her jaw dropped, and her eyes widened. She was wet and ready, already tightening herself around me, trying to pull me in deeper, but I was already reaching into her gut, not able to go any further. As I thrusted inside of her, my sack slapped against her ass, and she clung onto me, wrapping her hands around the back of my neck, throwing herself into each thrust, moaning into my ear.

Before I could cum, I slid out of her, and she threw herself onto her stomach. She crawled back towards the end of the bed and arched her back, putting her face into the covers as her hands spread upwards, her fingers crawling up the bedsheets as if she wanted to climb. I shoved in from behind, gripping her hips in my hands. She moaned louder and pushed herself into each thrust. The time was now. I stopped for one moment and she caught her breath.

"What are...you doing?" she asked, out of breath. "Why'd...you stop?" I grabbed the lube from beneath the bed and pushed her head back down into the bedsheets. She giggled, and I placed lube on my fingertips, then massaged across the crack of her tight ass. She jolted at first, and I thought she would stop me, but she kept still as I massaged.

"Do it," she said. She wanted to. She knew what I planned to do and gave me the green light. There wasn't any further room for failure. When she was lubed, I slowly put the tip in, and she spread her cheeks with her hands just as Melinda did. I might not have tried anal before Melinda, but something told me that Bryce had either done this before or simply knew what to do. When I was able to get all of me inside of her, I picked up the pace. It almost felt impossible to pull out of her because she was gripped around me so tight.

I felt myself getting ready to cum again. It rested right in the base of my sack and was funneling its way to the tip. Bryce thrusted against it, harder and faster than Melinda had. Her moans grew louder, and she spread her arms out on the bed. Then I heard my name threw her muffled cry and what she said after, allowed me to release and fill her up.

She said, "I'm cumming."

We lay in bed in silence. She kept my arms around her as I spooned her. Every now and then she would pull on my arms tighter and take a deep breath. I smiled at myself, able to give her what she's been wanting for the longest.

"I didn't know that's what you meant by spice things up, Jonathan. I've always wanted to try that, but didn't think you'd be into it."

"I'm glad I did," I told her. She turned and kissed me, then raised her hand.

"You know, this finger is naked." She wiggled her ring finger and smiled. "I think it's best you change that."

A Night with Paris

Chapter 1: The Gorilla

I sure love these slave auctions, the wooden platforms, the black horses pulling their carriages across the dirt paths, the fields of chocolate men pickin' and workin', bids held high in the air for the new ones that came fresh off the boat, and that smell. I sure love the smell of slave labor, sweat, and roasted peanuts.

I stand by my husband's carriage in a sundress every mornin' as he tries to make his bids. He told me it be best if I look better than most wives who come out to support their slave-ownin' husbands, but I don't like the other wives. They are snot-nosed, tea-drinkin', husband-gossipin,' floral-hat-wearin' donkeys. Their husbands are even worse.

But mine, Bubba, he's a persistent one, that man, still trying to find the perfect slave for our fields since two of the strong ones done got sick. Such a shame. I shook my head. They were sure good at their work. Ain't no way Bubba's gonna' find another fine, young, strong slave-like ones bedridden now.

The crowd of men throwin' their hands up at auction turned to an even bigger display of no-good manners and shovin'. They could barely keep themselves planted on the dirt, yellin' how much they'd take for this slave or that slave, could barely hear the one speakin' to 'em.

"Sold!" Two of the slaves stepped down off the wooden

platform, hands tied in rope, chains around their necks and ankles. They never let them wear shoes. Bubba told me it's in case one of them finds a ways to run free. Hard to get far runnin' through some woods barefoot. If a bullet or our dogs don't catch'em, it sure as hot hell would be a sharp rock in the heel of the foot, but I like the runners. The ones who spend years bein' loyal slaves, smilin' at us every mornin' and night, doin' real good work, to only one day make a run for them there woods.

The runners are the fit ones. They spend their times keepin' healthy, workin' out, and my favorite, them muscles. Ohhh, the body of them runners. More fit than the others. They care for themselves good, I'll say, but how's Bubba gonna' find any good boys in this rotten bunch off today's boat? I pouted and shook my head. As the next batch of slaves made their way up the platform, wearin' only brown, torn pants, Bubba made his way to the front. The crowd began to quiet itself for once. It was a strange thing for a crowd of men at auction become quiet, but when I glanced for myself, I learned why.

The three slaves lined themselves up before the men. The auctioneer told of two of the three boys and their prices, but when he got to the third, the increased price seemed more than worth it. Now, Bubba done made his bid on those two boys, and no one contested, but before he could make that mistake, I realized no one made a bid on the third slave, perhaps because they couldn't afford him. I reached into my pouch and seen the money I was carryin'. That alone was enough, but Bubba always said auctionin' was no place for a lady and to stay with the other wives. Before the auctioneer could sell those two boys to Bubba, I screamed as loud as I could.

"Wait!" Every face and head turned, and every child runnin' around stopped. The wives peered over and seized their gossipin' as I lifted my dress from the ground and hurried over in my white shoes across the dirt.

"Paris, ain't no need for you here," I heard Bubba say.

"Hear me out, dear." They parted from each other as I joined Bubba to the front. I peered up at the third boy no one bidded for, and he was a marvel. His chest was wide and beefy. His broad shoulders looked like he could carry my horses on them. His arms could build a foundation and a house without tools. Those thunderous thighs. My, oh my, if he made a run for it, I'd love to watch them muscles jiggle. I'd lick the sweat of his back, and if we had him, I could if I wanted to, and he wouldn't be able to do nothing about it. The slave peered down at me, and he was as calm as the quiet before a storm. His deep, brown eyes pierced into me.

"What are you doin', Paris? You should be back at the carriage with them horses." I stepped up the platform and found the slave to be the tallest of men all around us. He could block out the sun without tryin'. Make no mistake, if he were to trip over me, well, he just may flatten me out like coin. I reached to touch his shaved scalp, and he kept himself still. I don't think he blinked even. Some slaves tend to flinch when you reach for their face, but this one, he had no fear in his eyes. He didn't budge not one bit.

"What is his name?" I asked the auctioneer.

"This slave here, beautiful lady?" He peered over his spectacles at the slave then down at some papers. "His name here is Ape." I turned back to the slave and shook my head.

"Oh, no, you're mistaken. This ain't just not ape. We're lookin' at a gorilla."

"So, what say you?" Bubba asked the auctioneer. "I'll take these two boys?" I whipped to Bubba and kneeled on the platform before him.

"Can we have this one? Please, dear. This one."

"This boy? My, he's expensive."

"I have savin's." I showed him my pouch. Bubba sighed. It was the savin's he gave me for some time now. He was better than most husbands because anytime I requested somethin', he'd actually give it to me. That's why I married him over any other of the richer owners. "Please?" I asked again.

"You best take him," one of the other slave bidders said. "If I could afford that boy, I'd take him without another breath." Bubba thought for a moment, then smiled and nodded. He turned to the auctioneer.

"I've changed my mind. We'll take Ape."

"His name is Gorilla, Bubba." I turned to the slave and smiled. "Your name is Gorilla."

Chapter 2: Size Is Everything

When we got home, I couldn't keep my eyes off Gorilla. Those arms could carry me up and down the stairs, possibly around the entire plantation. What would there be a need for horses? I would only need Gorilla for that...and other things. As Gorilla was shown where he would sleep, Bubba led us back outside to the barn. The slaves picked in them fields and carried baskets of fruits from our gardens. The sun beat over us, and I already I felt my face getting clammy.

"Gorilla," I called. He glanced over his shoulder at me, and I had to toss my head back to look up at him. "The sun's blindin' me. Be my shade, would you?" Gorilla nodded and stepped to the side, blockin' the sun out as Bubba unlocked the barn. He went inside and came back out with some papers. He fumbled through them until he came to a stop.

"Gorilla, you's got some good laboring here in your file. With your--" And Bubba stopped and examined him, "--build, I'd say you'll make quite a fine field slave."

"But dear, wouldn't he make a better house slave?" I pleaded. Bubba frowned and shook his head.

"Do you not see how big this here boy is, Paris?" He scratched the top of his baldin' whiskered head then put his hat back on. The other bidders always tried to make a pass at me, sayin' I was far too beautiful for a man like Bubba. I was, but I liked Bubba for one reason: He gave me anything I asked for. That's the man you marry.

"Oh, trust me, I do," I said, examinin' Gorilla from head to toe.

"Then won't you agree that he'd be best for harder labor. He could carry and pick twice as much as everyone else." I pouted and turned away.

"You always decide. Can't I decide ever?" Bubba sighed, and I knew my persuasion worked.

"Alright, alright, Paris. Don't be sad, you hear? Gorilla. You're a house slave. Do whatever my wife needs, and there won't be no need for me to teach you a thing or two." I waited for Gorilla to respond, but he nodded again.

"Don't he talk?" I asked. Bubba shook his head.

"Said in his papers that Gorilla don't talk. He does exactly as he's told. No questions asked. Has no history of making a run for it. Almost like this boy was destined to slave. Others can learn or thing or two from his file...if they could read." Gorilla not being able to talk only made everythin' much easier for me. That meant Gorilla could keep secrets, and as dumb as a nail my husband was, I could say anything to Gorilla, and he'd not find out about it.

"You don't say?" Bubba nodded and walked back towards the house. Gorilla stood before me, watching him leave. When I heard the white door close behind Bubba, I examined Gorilla more. "You heard him?" I asked.

Gorilla looked confused for a moment, then glanced at the house before givin' me his attention again. I walked circles around him, runnin' my hand across his chest, then back before grabbin' a handful of his sack and cock. To my surprise, I couldn't tell if he was already this hard and big, but whichever he was, I could barely wrap my hand around his cock completely. Big as a gorilla and hung like a horse.

"You must do whatever I need." He frowned a bit, then took a step back. "I think you'll like it here, Gorilla. I really think you will."

~

As Gorilla prepared supper with the other house slaves, Bubba and I took our places at the table. It was rather different having a slave his size in the kitchen. The other slaves kept themselves distant from him, probably thinkin' his presence in the house only meant he was a snitch to watch over them.

"Is it ready?" Bubba asked the slaves. In a moment, four of our female slaves walked in a single line, each holding a bowl.

"Massa'," one of them said as they placed the bowls in front of us. "Gorilla won't make what we tells him. Gorilla kept makin' stew as we made chicken. We told him not to do that. I says, 'Massa' won't like you changing his food. Massa' like chicken on Wednesdays,' and Gorilla, he--"

Bubba raised his hand. "It is fine," he told her. "Just, it better be good. Gorilla, bring yourself in here." Gorilla walked in. "Why you don't make what they make, Gorilla? You made this stew?"

Gorilla nodded. "Well, it best be good, boy."

They laid the bowl before us, and the aroma that settled in my nose was the most pleasant smell all summer. There were steamed, mixed vegetables swimming in a beef, meaty broth. There were snipped pieces of sausages too.

"It does smell great, Gorilla," I said, and Bubba nodded. He took a sip, and when he turned to Gorilla, he smiled.

"Boy, that is a mighty fine bowl of stew. You best teach them something in there." Gorilla smiled and nodded. When he looked over at me, I ran my tongue across my lips, then smiled. His smile faded. As big as Gorilla was, I felt he was afraid of me, but I couldn't blame him. As Bubba finished his meal, he ordered Gorilla to go upstairs and bathe himself in good soap as his reward.

I followed Gorilla up the stairs and to the bathroom. When I got to the door, I peeked through the hole and seen the snake he was carryin' behind them torn pants. I opened the door, and he jolted, bringin' one of the towels around him.

"No need to be started, Gorilla." I stepped into the bathroom and closed the door behind me. "Move that towel out of the way. You're blocking the view." Gorilla hesitated for a while, but then his eyes trailed to the floor. He removed the towel, and when it hit the floor, my jaw fell with it.

"My, oh my, Gorilla. What big...cock, you have." He mustered a smile. "Ahhh, there it is. That white smile." It faded. I took a step forward, and he kept himself grounded where he stood. "Now, there is no need to be afraid, Gorilla. I'm not tryin' to purposely get you into trouble. I only wanted to see you...All of you." I gripped his cock in my hand and started caressing it. He shut his eyes and breathed steadily. "See you like it. That's a good boy." I then got on my knees and gave him a suckin', tonguin' around his thick, black stallion. He stumbled back against the sink, and I stopped. His eyes widened, and he lifted his towel from the floor.

"I'm sorry I startled you," I told him. "I like you, Gorilla." The shock in his eyes began to fade. I pulled down the shoulder straps of my sundress and let him see my perky, pink breasts. "Do you like what you see?" His eyes widened again, and he rose off the bathroom sink. He began to nod endlessly. I grabbed his hands and let him touched them. He jolted for a moment, but when he saw that I was only being fair to let him touch me too, he relaxed.

"Do you like me?" He nodded again. As he held my breasts and started to caress them, I removed my undergarments and balled them into my fist. I held them up to his face. "This is the password to my room if you dare wish to enter when my husband takes his leave tomorrow."

I pulled the straps back over my breasts and fixed my dress. "Now, you enjoy your washing."

Chapter 3: A Trick or a Treat

The next mornin', Bubba got them horses ready and hopped into the carriage. The field slaves had been given their work as the house slaves cleaned up and made breakfast with Gorilla.

"I'll be back tomorrow mornin', hopefully with another field slave since you took Gorilla," Bubba said. "You sure you don't want to come this time? You always want to come. I could see to it that my brother come watch these slaves for me again. He's only down the path."

"I'll be fine here, dear. No need having Joshua come once more. I'll watch over them." Bubba studied me for a moment, then nodded.

"Well, alright. You have Gorilla help keep them all in line. That's our muscle there. Have them clean that barn."

"I'll take care of everythin', and you just go on now to your auction." Bubba nodded and I kissed him on his cheek. I watched him as he headed down the path and listened until I could no longer hear the horses gallop. Finally, that man left me alone. Only time he doesn't listen to me is when he wants to climb his heavy self atop of me at night. I needed a real man to please. With Bubba gone until morning, make no mistake, I was going to be a changed woman by then.

I went back into the house and headed for the bedroom. I removed my shoes, fluffed the pillows, and prepared the bed. Could the bed even hold with Gorilla on it? It was impossible to figure out, but we might as well find out together. It felt like I had laid in the bed forever, waitin' for Gorilla to come up the stairs and climb in with me. I was getting impatient. Surely, Gorilla would know I wanted him to come up now without me tellin' him to. I grew tired of waitin' for him. I realized he obviously didn't understand me last night, and when I peered out the window, I saw him in the fields workin'.

Now, this angered me. Gorilla had no business in them fields. His business was with me in this bed until I tell him otherwise. But he was there, clear as day, sweatin' beneath the boiling hot sun, pickin' the cotton in them fields. I threw my sundress back on and stammered down the steps. When I stomped down the front steps, the plantation froze. My eyes blazed straight to Gorilla. As everyone else stopped workin' as I passed, Gorilla had no idea I was comin' for him. He was goin' to get it. He was goin' to get what he asked for.

"Gorilla," I said, as calmly as I could. He turned his head towards me and stared blankly. "What are you doin' out here in these fields? You's a house-slave. You ain't no field-slave." Gorilla shook his head. "You tellin' me no, Gorilla? You tellin' me, no?" He didn't respond. "Go back in the house."

He sighed and kept pickin'. My anger burst from my throat as I smacked his bare, sweating back. "Go back to the house!" He stopped and frowned. I pointed at the house, and he followed with his eyes. When my voice disappeared across the fields, he stopped working and started walkin' back towards the house. I thought yellin' at him finally got him to listen, but I was wrong. Gorilla didn't go back to the house, and instead, he went to the barn.

"I said house, Gorilla! Not barn!" I didn't feel good about yellin' at Gorilla, but he just wasn't listenin' to me. With Bubba gone, who knew what Gorilla had planned. I might have felt safe with Bubba here, but without Bubba's voice, Gorilla felt he could do as he pleased. Perhaps he could have, as long as one of them things wasn't leavin' the plantation. Gorilla pulled the barn door from its hinges. His strength frightened me, and I realized he, too, was angry. "Gorilla, what is the matter with you?"

He shuffled through the papers in the barn and grabbed Bubba's writin' tool. He began to write on the back of the papers vigorously, then he pressed the paper against my chest. I had not known Gorilla knew how to read and write.

:You trickin' me into a hanging.:

I shook my head. "Oh, no, Gorilla, this is no trick. I wouldn't do that to you. You are my favorite." He wrote again on another paper.

:How do I know this is no trick?:
I ripped the papers up, and he frowned. I stepped forward and reached for the sides of his face. He caught me by the wrists, then stared at me for a while.

Eventually, he released me and allowed me to caress his face with my hands.

"Because I'm going to show you this isn't a trick." I looked over my shoulder, and when my glare reached across the fields and the house, the slaves went back to work. I took Gorilla by the hand and led him into the barn. Gorilla grabbed the door and propped it enough to close us in. I prepared the haystacks as Gorilla stood by the barn doors and watched. When I was finished, I stood up and held out my hand for him to come forward. He hesitated, but eventually, he put his trust in me.

I took him by the hand and led him to the center of the barn. He stood as still as a statue, but I kept goin'. My dress dropped to the ground and joined the hay beneath my shoes. The sunlight squeezed between the cracks of the wooden barn walls, and the light formed stripes against my naked body.

"You ever been with a woman before, Gorilla?" He gazed at my physique, and I traced my fingers between my breasts and ran my fingers down to my inner thighs and caressed across my hips. He shook his head. "Well, I'm honored to be your first…If you'd let me." His adam's apple rose and sunk within his throat as he nodded.

I approached him slowly, steppin' over my dress and shoes. I kissed his full lips and ran my fingers up his massive forearms and biceps. When I got to his shoulders, I just couldn't contain myself any longer, but since it was his first time, I wanted to make it worth his while. I squatted before him and pushed him up against one of the haystacks. He stood against it as I removed his brown pants. I ran my hands along his meaty thighs, his cock swung back in forth before my face. He was as big as my head.

I took him in my grasp and jerked him slowly. Couldn't get a full grip around him, but enough for him to enjoy it. He pushed his head back and stared up at the ceilin'. I took him into my mouth. Had to stretch it wide quite a bit just to fit him in. He hardened by the second, and I couldn't possibly believe that he was growin' in my throat. I sucked and bobbed and used my fingers to play with his sack. It might have tickled him at first, for when I first did it, I thought I heard him chuckle, and when he did, it made his cock flex into my mouth, and I almost gagged. I used my hands some more and gave his cock a good spit to wet it up. Then I led him back to the center of the floor.

"Lie on your back," I told him. He listened, keepin' his gaze on me, and he didn't hesitate this time. He sounded as if he was tryin' to catch his breath, but that's just the type of excitement you find in boys. He might not have been a young virgin, but he sure had the heart of one. I stood over him as he lay back and cock stood straight up. "This isn't my first time, I can tell you that, Gorilla. Not with a slave either. I know you'll like this. The one before you did too."

I squatted above him, and he kept his hands at his side. He might not have known what to do, but that's why I had him lie there like that. Didn't have no need for him to move. I held my squat just above his cock and grabbed hold of it. I slowly inched down onto it, putting the tip of it inside. He stretched me from the beginning. I had to slow myself down. He was as girthy as a whale. As I inched him deep inside of me, it throbbed like a heartbeat. He tensed up real good. I moaned over him, still makin' my way down to his sack, but that's when the virgin in him died. He pushed his cock upward and shoved himself in. I was more than wet enough for him to get in with ease, but I wasn't deep enough for all of him to get inside. It felt like he jabbed my stomach, and it forced me to hop up for a moment and take a breath.

"This is going to be harder than I thought, Gorilla...You are something, you know that?" He smiled, but at least he was enjoying himself. Big slave boy like him needed someone like me for an experience. I squatted again, only this time, I was able to fit more of him. I felt stuffed as I rode him. A pleasurable pressure, then a release of it over and over. I covered his cock with my woman juice. It sounded like splashin' water. As I rode Gorilla, I kept one hand gripped around his cock, giving it a squeeze every time I went up, just to slam myself back down. Eventually, those massive hands moved. He placed his hands beneath my ass and held one cheek in each hand. It fit perfectly as if my ass was made for his grip. My cheeks fit like a small ball in his hand as he guided the pace.

When I came the second time on Gorilla, he changed things up on me. He was no longer into takin' orders and instead took matters into his own two hands. He picked me up off the floor and held me up over him. I placed my legs over his shoulders and around his face, and he ate me like he hadn't had supper in weeks. His tongue almost felt as big as his cock, slitherin' inside of me like a snake. I was high enough to grab hold of one of the barn's wooden planks above. He kept my ass gripped in his hands.

When he was finished, he pulled me down and bent me over the haystacks. I wasn't sure where he learned this before, but perhaps, there was a man in him after all besides looking like one. He shoved himself in, and I almost sprang over the hay. It both hurt and felt wonderful, and once he built up a nice, even pace, I rested myself on the hay and ran my fingers through it. Gorilla explored every part of me with his hands, runnin' them down my back and spine, then up my sides, then grabbin' handfuls of my hair. He grunted like an animal, and I thought the barn would collapse from the force he was puttin' into me. I couldn't take anymore, but Gorilla wanted to keep goin'.

I collapsed on the hay, tryin' to take the pleasure and pain all at once. He grunted and grunted, and grunted, and thrusted, and thrusted, and thrusted. As I came on him again, I let out a scream but shoved my hand over my mouth so the other slaves wouldn't think Gorilla was attemptin' to kill me. He threw his back into a final thrust, and I felt a warm pool of his cum inside of me. He stumbled back, and each breath he took would have blown the hay around the barn. I couldn't move. I couldn't catch my breath. All I could do is just lie there, still bent over, vulnerable, and exposed. I only hoped Gorilla was satisfied enough to not plunder me again.

But then I heard gallopin'. Make no mistake, horses were comin' back to the plantation. I sprang up from the hay, and Gorilla pushed the hay away to find his pants. Once I got my dress on, I fixed up my hair, and put my shoes on. I had to take them off and put them on the right foot. Gorilla stood ready to walk out the barn. He surely built up a sweat, and so did I. By the time Gorilla moved the barn door out of the way, Bubba's carriage came to a stop. He peered over at Gorilla and me and squinted his eyes. He then hopped out of his carriage and hustled over as Gorilla helped me out of the barn.

"Paris?" Bubba called. "What is that house slave doing--- outside the house?" Gorilla looked afraid. I know he must've thought he'd be in trouble, but I knew Bubba more than Gorilla. Gorilla gave me the saddest eyes. I've never seen such fear in a man's eyes before.

"I went to the barn because I thought I heard someone scream, so I hurried out here and look, dear. The door. Someone might have came into our barn, and I was scared!" I mustered myself a good cry, turnin' away from Bubba and facin' Gorilla. "But Gorilla came, and I think Gorilla might have scared whoever it was away. You see, dear. Gorilla is a good slave. That's why I wanted to keep him close. I told you so, dear. I told you we'd do good buyin' him." Bubba examined the barn door and peered at Gorilla.

"That true, Gorilla?" he asked. "You saved my wife." I stared at Gorilla, and he glanced at me then glanced at Bubba. He nodded. Bubba sprang to life and patted him endlessly on his bare back.

"Well, let's head inside to celebrate! You worked up a sweat now, didn't you, boy?! Haha! Saved my dear Paris when I'm not here! Now, that's a fine boy!" Bubba rushed to the house and ushered all the slaves on the plantation inside. I peered up at Gorilla then rested my hand on his cheek.

"You're a good boy, Gorilla. I imagine you want to do it again sometime, don't you?" Gorilla nodded. "Good. As do I, my Gorilla. As do I."